You're About to Become a

Pr... *Woman.*

INTRODUCING
PAGES & PRIVILEGES™.

It's our way of thanking you for buying
our books at your favorite retail store.

— *Get all this Free* —

WITH JUST ONE PROOF OF PURCHASE:

◆ Hotel Discounts up to 60% at home and abroad

◆ Travel Service - Guaranteed lowest published
   airfares plus 5% cash back on tickets

◆ $25 Travel Voucher

◆ Sensuous Petite Parfumerie collection ($50 value)

◆ Insider Tips Letter with sneak previews of
   upcoming books

◆ Mystery Gift (if you enroll before 6/15/95)

You'll get a FREE personal card, too.
It's your passport to all these benefits— and to
even more great gifts & benefits to come!

There's no club to join. No purchase commitment. No obligation.

As a Privileged Woman,
you'll be entitled to all these Free Benefits. And Free Gifts, too.

To thank you for buying our books, we've designed an exclusive FREE program called *PAGES & PRIVILEGES*™. You can enroll with just one Proof of Purchase, and get the kind of luxuries that, until now, you could only read about.

BIG HOTEL DISCOUNTS

A privileged woman stays in the finest hotels. And so can you—at up to 60% off! Imagine standing in a hotel check-in line and watching as the guest in front of you pays $150 for the same room that's only costing you $60. Your *Pages & Privileges* discounts are good at Sheraton, Marriott, Best Western, Hyatt and thousands of other fine hotels all over the U.S., Canada and Europe.

FREE DISCOUNT TRAVEL SERVICE

A privileged woman is always jetting to romantic places. When <u>you</u> fly, just make one phone call for the lowest published airfare at time of booking—<u>or double the difference back</u>! PLUS—

you'll get a $25 voucher to use the first time you book a flight AND <u>5% cash back on every ticket you buy thereafter through the travel service</u>!

*F*REE GIFTS!

A privileged woman is always getting wonderful gifts.
Luxuriate in rich fragrances that will stir your senses (and his). This gift-boxed assortment of fine perfumes includes three popular scents, each in a beautiful designer bottle. <u>Truly Lace</u>...This luxurious fragrance unveils your sensuous side. <u>L'Effleur</u>...discover the romance of the Victorian era with this soft floral. <u>Muguet des bois</u>...a single note floral of singular beauty. This $50 value is yours—FREE when you enroll in *Pages & Privileges*! And it's just the beginning of the gifts and benefits that will be coming your way!

$50 VALUE

*F*REE INSIDER TIPS LETTER

A privileged woman is always informed. And you'll be, too, with our free letter full of fascinating information and sneak previews of upcoming books.

*M*ORE GREAT GIFTS & BENEFITS TO COME

A privileged woman always has a lot to look forward to.
And so will you. You get all these wonderful FREE gifts and benefits now with only one purchase...and there are no additional purchases required. However, each additional retail purchase of Harlequin and Silhouette books brings you a step closer to even more great FREE benefits like half-price movie tickets...and even more FREE gifts like these beautiful fragrance gift baskets:

L'Effleur ...This basketful of romance lets you discover L'Effleur from head to toe, heart to home.

Truly Lace ...A basket spun with the sensuous luxuries of Truly Lace, including Dusting Powder in a reusable satin and lace covered box.

*E*NROLL *N*OW!
Complete the Enrollment Form on the back of this card and become a Privileged Woman today!

Enroll Today in *PAGES & PRIVILEGES*™, the program that gives you Great Gifts and Benefits with just one purchase!

Enrollment Form

☐ *Yes!* I WANT TO BE A *Privileged Woman.*

Enclosed is one *PAGES & PRIVILEGES*™ Proof of Purchase from any Harlequin or Silhouette book currently for sale in stores (Proofs of Purchase are found on the back pages of books) and the store cash register receipt. Please enroll me in *PAGES & PRIVILEGES*™. Send my Welcome Kit and FREE Gifts -- and activate my FREE benefits -- immediately.

NAME (please print)

ADDRESS   APT. NO

CITY   STATE   ZIP/POSTAL CODE

PROOF OF PURCHASE

Please allow 6-8 weeks for delivery. Quantities are limited. We reserve the right to substitute items. Enroll before October 31, 1995 and receive one full year of benefits.

NO CLUB!
NO COMMITMENT!
Just one purchase brings you great Free Gifts and Benefits!
(See inside for details.)

Name of store where this book was purchased_____

Date of purchase_____

Type of store:

☐ Bookstore   ☐ Supermarket   ☐ Drugstore

☐ Dept. or discount store (e.g. K-Mart or Walmart)

☐ Other (specify)_____

Which Harlequin or Silhouette series do you usually read?

_____

Complete and mail with one Proof of Purchase and store receipt to:

U.S.: *PAGES & PRIVILEGES*™, P.O. Box 1960, Danbury, CT 06813-1960

Canada: *PAGES & PRIVILEGES*™, 49-6A The Donway West, P.O. 813, North York, ON M3C 2E8   PRINTED IN U.S.A

Chrissy heard Blaze speaking...every word was crystal clear

"When I say *nouveau riche* I mean *nouveau riche*. The Hamiltons were into spotlit bonsai trees and floodlit oils..."

Chrissy straightened and froze.

"The mother was the worm that turned. Belle drank too much and dropped the most frightful clangers with the happiest smiles. When the good life got too much she ran off with a freezer salesman, who turned out to be a bigamist—"

Chrissy had the vase of wilted flowers in her hand. He was indolently sprawled on the sofa several steps inside the door. Chrissy upended the contents over Blaze Kenyon's gleaming dark head.

LYNNE GRAHAM was born in Northern Ireland and has been a keen reader of romance since her teens. She is happily married, with an understanding husband who has learned to cook since she started to write! Her three children, two of whom are adopted, keep her on her toes. She also has a very large wolfhound, who knocks over everything with her tail, and an even more adored mongrel, who rules everybody. When time allows, Lynne is a keen gardener and loves experimenting with Italian cookery.

Books by Lynne Graham

HARLEQUIN PRESENTS
1551—TEMPTESTUOUS REUNION
1696—A VENGEFUL PASSION
1712—ANGEL OF DARKNESS

LYNNE GRAHAM

Indecent Deception

Harlequin Books

TORONTO • NEW YORK • LONDON
AMSTERDAM • PARIS • SYDNEY • HAMBURG
STOCKHOLM • ATHENS • TOKYO • MILAN
MADRID • WARSAW • BUDAPEST • AUCKLAND

ISBN 0-373-11740-X

INDECENT DECEPTION

Copyright © 1994 by Lynne Graham.

First North American Publication 1995.

This edition published by arrangement with Harlequin Enterprises B.V.

Printed in U.S.A.

CHAPTER ONE

CHRISSY leapt off the bus and splashed straight into a puddle. Dirty water spattered the pristine overall she wore beneath her unbuttoned coat. With a groan of exasperation she fled on down the road, frantically checking her watch. She was late for work.

As she dived across a narrow side-street, the screech of brakes almost deafened her. Jerking round, she had a brief blurred image of the car bearing down on her before she lost her balance and landed with her behind and her two hands braced on the wet tarmac. Winded and shocked, she just sat there dazedly appreciating that she was still in one piece. The glossy black bonnet of the luxury sports car was less than a foot from her face.

A car door slammed. A pair of male feet shod in handstitched Italian leather entered her vision. 'You stupid, crazy little idiot!'

There was something disorientatingly familiar about that clipped well-bred drawl that voiced abuse with lacerating cool. Her wide green eyes climbed up the long straight length of masculine legs sheathed in the mohair blend of bespoke tailoring.

'Well,' the same objectionable voice continued, 'what have you got to say for yourself?'

Chrissy's dilated gaze swept over a flat, taut stomach and mounted a scarlet silk tie that lent flamboyance to a superbly cut navy suit, and there her head tipped back on her shoulders, impatience spurring her on to confirm her suspicions.

'Maybe I ran over your tongue...'

Her tongue did have a problem. Disbelief had glued it to the roof of her mouth. Blaze Kenyon. Breathtaking, unforgettable and utterly unmistakable for anyone else.

He was incredibly good-looking and soul-destroyingly unattainable unless, Chrissy had once noted, your beauty was on a par with his. Once long ago, in a purely philosophical mood, Chrissy had wondered why beautiful men were invariably attracted only to equally beautiful women.

Indeed, until Blaze parted his lips and actually spoke, he was so dazzlingly perfect that you were tempted to pinch him to see if he was real. As his luxuriant black hair ruffled in the breeze, Chrissy was briefly inspected by brilliant sapphire-blue eyes.

Hitching his knife-creased trousers, he crouched down to run a pair of excruciatingly thorough hands over her extended limbs in search of injury.

'I suppose you do realise that you're sitting in a puddle.' Suddenly he smiled, brilliantly, blindingly. He had the sort of charisma that switched on like a high-voltage searchlight, targeting a victim. When he switched it off again, it was a little like being plunged into outer darkness.

Careless long brown fingers were still anchored to her slim thigh. Chrissy unfroze and thrust the over-familiar hand violently away. It was not a reaction Blaze was accustomed to receiving. A slight frownline was etched between his winged dark brows as he sprang up again.

She stumbled clumsily upright on knees that didn't feel strong enough to support her entire weight.

Blaze didn't even recognise her. Sudden bitter resentment thrust Chrissy's chin up. 'You could've k-killed me!' she condemned. 'You were driving f-far too fast.'

'Good God,' Blaze breathed softly, studying her truculent, defensive face. 'It's Chrissy.'

'C-Christabel,' she corrected coldly, cursing the stammer that often dogged her in moments of stress.

Blaze ran a measuring scrutiny over her, taking in dirty hands, laddered tights and curling mahogany streamers of flyaway hair descending forlornly from an inexpert topknot. 'You haven't changed,' he said.

Scarlet to her hairline, Chrissy squashed an embarrassing urge to point out what she felt should have been obvious even to the most disinterested observer. Over the past three years, she had shed almost three stone. 'N-neither have you,' she countered with fierce sincerity.

His forefinger flicked the Peter Pan collar of her overall. 'Are you a nurse now?' His tone was dubious.

'Why should you be interested?' she slung between clenched teeth, fighting her stammer with all her might, and that generally made it worse.

'Mere curiosity? I wasn't expecting to meet a Hamilton today,' Blaze supplied very, very coolly. 'Are you sure you're not hurt?'

'I doubt if you'd care whether I was or not.' Chrissy clung to her hostility as though it were a suit of armour.

'You've only bruised your pride and your backside.' A teasing edge had softened his clipped vowels.

A second earlier she had been wondering at the icy edge to his tone when he voiced her surname, but now that was forgotten as her teeth ground together. It might have been three years since she last saw him, but Blaze Kenyon still affected her much as a whip would laid across her sensitive flesh. 'I have to get to work,' she enunciated with stiff dignity. 'N-nice meeting you again.'

Blaze roared with laughter. 'Nice meeting me? I damned near ran over you! You should think twice before you throw yourself beneath my wheels.'

'I did not *throw myself*——' Chrissy began furiously.

'Fortunately I have fast reflexes,' Blaze murmured reflectively, choosing to concentrate on that aspect of the episode rather than the shock she had sustained.

'I have to get to work,' Chrissy repeated with wooden emphasis, and without another word she walked away with a ramrod-straight back, seethingly conscious of the amused sapphire eyes following in her wake. She ached to massage a certain throbbing portion of her anatomy, but she fought the need until she had entered the exclusive apartment block several yards away and knew herself safely out of sight. Her coat was sodden. She was soaked to the skin.

'What happened to you?' A slender blonde, clad in a matching overall, answered her urgent knock on the door of one of the ground-floor apartments and gaped at her bedraggled appearance.

'I fell,' Chrissy gasped, open prayer on her feverishly flushed features. 'Have you got anything I could borrow?'

'Sorry... you're supposed to carry a spare overall of your own,' Glynis reminded her, looking superior.

'I just can't afford to buy another one this month. I wash this one out every night.'

'Working a lying month is the pits,' Glynis remarked without great interest as she cast herself down on a richly upholstered sofa and switched on the television with a flick of the remote-control.

'Did Mr Cranmore phone?' Chrissy was dabbing ineffectually at the stains on her overall with a handful of tissues. It would be just her luck if this was one of the days their mutual employer decided to do a spot check on one of his newest workers.

'Relax,' Glynis groaned. 'You worry too much.'

'Shouldn't we be getting started?'

'Run a vacuum over the place. That's all it needs,' Glynis advised, lighting up a cigarette and showing no sign of movement. 'I don't know why a couple as clean as this bother to use a cleaning agency...'

'Do you think you should be smoking here?' Chrissy prompted uncomfortably on her passage to the cupboard where the vacuum was kept.

'I deserve a break like anybody else.'

If Martin Cranmore found anyone else slacking on the job, it would mean instant dismissal. But he had a soft spot for Glynis. Glynis had baby-blue eyes and fluffy blonde hair and they licensed her to get away with murder. The other cleaners hated her. None of the other women wanted to partner Glynis. The blonde never did her share of the work and, if there was a complaint, Chrissy had already been warned that it would not be Glynis who took the blame for it.

Chrissy had been employed by the Silent Sweep agency for just three weeks and she was desperate to hang on to her job. The cleaning agency had a rulebook a full half-inch thick, and within the space of one working day Chrissy had watched the blonde break every rule in it. The ultimate sin was to make oneself at home in a client's apartment. There was a strictly regimented list of tasks to be carried out on every visit...and those tasks were to be done even if they did not appear to be necessary. That was what the client was paying for. Silent, unseen service.

Blaze Kenyon. As Chrissy whizzed about with the vacuum, he leapt into her mind the instant she was free to think about him. He exploded out of her carefully blocked subconscious with the shock value of an evil genie. In his wake came a tidal wave of homesickness and a surge of very painful memories.

She was able to suppress the homesickness. After all, she no longer had a home worthy of sentimental recall, she reminded herself. Not only was her mother dead and her siblings married, but Chrissy herself was all too wretchedly aware that, no matter how bad things got, she could never expect her father to house her again.

The painful memories were far more resilient. Out there on the street, Blaze had committed the ultimate sin of seeing her as she used to be. The Hamilton family misfit. Elaine's overweight, socially inadequate kid sister. Did he even remember his last encounter with Chrissy Hamilton? She shuddered at the very idea of him remembering. No, he wouldn't remember. A bottle of whisky on top of a recent family bereavement had made him more than usually callous and indifferent to the feelings of others. Humiliating Elaine's kid sister had cost him not a pang of conscience. He had been incredibly cruel, so cruel that Chrissy still carried the scars.

Glynis screened a yawn as they entered the third-floor apartment next on their schedule. Chrissy headed straight for the kitchen and stopped dead on the threshold. 'Oh, hell!' she muttered in dismay, absorbing the devastation before her.

Glynis swore at the sight of the abandoned dishes piled high on every surface and the smell of stale food. 'She's had a party and left us to clear it up. Well, she can forget that!' she said aggressively.

'We're down for two hours extra here. Now we know why.' Chrissy opened a window to air the room. 'I'll start in here, shall I? You can take the lounge,' she suggested.

Glynis said something rude and stalked off. Chrissy worked quietly and efficiently, hoping that just for once Glynis was in the mood for work. Their schedule had to be strictly followed. Clients always specified hours when their homes were empty.

'What do you think?'

Chrissy spun and her eyes widened incredulously. Glynis was doing a twirl in a fancy cocktail dress.

'Couldn't resist it...gorgeous, isn't it? And she'll never notice. The bedroom's a tip. This was lying on the floor——'

'For heaven's sake, take it off and put it back!' Chrissy gasped in horror.

'Don't be such a pain!' Glynis groaned. 'I've done the lounge. I'll finish up in here if you like. I hate doing corner baths...'

'Take it off!' Chrissy repeated.

Glynis gave her a filthy look. 'OK...OK. I can't say you're a barrel of fun to work with, can I?' she snapped.

Chrissy had just entered the bathroom when she heard the front door open and the sound of voices, male and female mingling. She sprang upright, wondering frantically if Glynis had had time to change back into her overall. A brunette appeared in the doorway and frowned. 'Aren't you finished yet?'

'I'm sorry, no.' Chrissy made no attempt to point out that they had been booked for a specified time and were indeed still half an hour within that period. 'Do you want us to leave?'

The elegant brunette pouted. 'How long will it take you to finish up?'

'About twenty minutes...'

'I suppose I'll have to put up with you, then, or I won't be getting what I paid for,' the brunette said witheringly.

'Who are you talking to?' a dismayingly familiar drawl interposed.

Blaze Kenyon strolled into view.

'What are you doing h-here?' Chrissy demanded in stark disbelief, her faith in the impossibility of two such glaring coincidences in one day severely shaken.

His brilliant blue eyes narrowed. 'I was about to pick Leila up when we ran into each other earlier. What are you doing in her bathroom——?'

'She's supposed to be cleaning it!' his female companion cut in thinly. 'Are you telling me that you *know* this girl?'

'You're a cleaner?' Blaze did not conceal his astonishment.

Leila curved a hand round his arm. 'Come on, darling... the sooner she finishes, the quicker she'll be out of here,' she purred suggestively, but she eyed Chrissy with grim annoyance.

Chrissy felt utterly humiliated. She was not ashamed of what she did for a living. The hours suited her and the agency paid a reasonable rate. Three years ago she would never have dreamt that she would be cleaning other people's homes to survive, but a lot of things had changed in those same three years. She had no false pride about her work, had indeed been grateful to have paid employment...until Blaze Kenyon surveyed her with well-bred amazement and suddenly made her feel like the lowest of the low.

'Hell, that was close!' Glynis whispered from the doorway. 'I'll finish the kitchen. You dump those flowers in the hall and we'll get out!'

Chrissy was gathering the fallen petals off the carpet when she heard Blaze speaking. The lounge door wasn't closed and he had a deep, carrying voice. Every word was crystal-clear.

'When I say *nouveau riche* I mean *nouveau riche*. The Hamiltons were into spotlit bonsai trees and floodlit oils. Jim Hamilton is one of the most vulgar loudmouths one could meet...'

Chrissy straightened and froze, her facial muscles clenching painfully tight as she moved closer to the ajar door, the sound of her own ruptured breathing loud in her eardrums.

'The mother was the worm that turned,' Blaze drawled smoothly. 'Belle was quite incapable of furthering Hamilton's social aspirations. She drank too much and dropped the most frightful clangers with the happiest smiles. When the good life got too much, she ran off with a freezer salesman, who turned out to be a bigamist. Hamilton thought it was the funniest thing he had ever heard. Night after night he dined out on the story with glee——'

'What are you doing?' Glynis demanded from behind her as Chrissy thrust the door wide.

Chrissy had the vase of wilted flowers in her hand. Blaze was indolently sprawled on the sofa several steps inside the door. Raising the vase, Chrissy up-ended the contents over Blaze Kenyon's gleaming dark head.

Leila shrieked as though she had plunged a knife into his back. The vase contained a surprising amount of water. A deluge descended on Chrissy's victim.

Blaze sprang up, scattering flowers, and spun round.

'You p-pig!' Chrissy shouted.

Blaze clawed wet hair off his brow with one hand, his glittering ice-blue eyes smouldering threat at Chrissy.

'You are a p-pig!' Without warning her bravado was punctured.

'Are you crazy?' the brunette screamed at her shrilly.

'Angry,' Blaze murmured drily.

'I'm going to have you fired for this!' Leila promised, grabbing up the phone and punching out a number.

Glynis came running with a towel and fervent apologies.

Chrissy stood there blinking in bewilderment. But inside her head she was still hearing Blaze slice her parents to ribbons, serving up her poor mother's heartbreak as a grotesque source of entertainment. He was a filthy, rotten snob! Born with the proverbial silver spoon in his mouth, grandson of an earl, Blaze had grown up against a background of rich, inherited privilege. His arrogance was that of an aristocrat, who had never known what it was to try and measure up to the expectations of a higher social class.

'Your boss wants to speak to you!' The smiling brunette extended the receiver like a hangman extending the noose.

On wooden legs, Chrissy stepped forward. Martin Cranmore was practically sobbing with rage at the other end of the line. What he said was short and sweet. Whitefaced and trembling, Chrissy looked at no one as she turned and walked out of the room. She gathered up her coat and bag.

Glynis caught her arm, oozing morbid fascination. 'What the hell did you do it for? Do you know who that gorgeous hunk is?'

Pulling on her coat, Chrissy said nothing.

'He's that racehorse trainer! He's the one with all the women, practically a harem from what you read in the papers!' Glynis gushed excitedly.

The sheer incredulity on Blaze's sun-bronzed features swam before her afresh. In retrospect, she could barely believe what she had done. He had probably never been assaulted by flowers before. Nervous husbands and protective fathers avoided his company. Around thirty most men settled down. Blaze hadn't. Scandal still shadowed his every step and no doubt he reacted with sublime insouciance to all rumour and report. His hide was tough. She would not have embarrassed him. And an hour from now he would be cracking a joke about it in that mocking, sardonic way of his.

But Chrissy would not be laughing. She had just sacrificed her job, and her job had been the one little bit of security she had left. The last piece of her mother's jewellery had been sold three months ago. The proceeds were long gone. She was stony broke and behind with her rent. She had practically pleaded with Martin Cranmore to give her the job. Desperation had overcome pride. That job had given her hope. She had seen it as a first basic foothold on survival.

And now it was gone, and with it the wages due to her for the past three weeks. Loyalty was all very well when you could afford it, Chrissy conceded painfully, but she hadn't been able to afford the cost of emptying that vase over Blaze Kenyon's arrogant head. A sense of utter desolation crept over her. Dear God, what was she going to do now? How were they to survive?

It was raining heavily. With a bent head she crossed the street and began walking. Digging her hands into her pockets, she didn't even try to avoid the puddles. When a car door shot open in front of her, she recoiled in alarm.

'Get in!' Blaze instructed abrasively. 'And take off that filthy coat first!'

Chrissy gaped in at him across a divide of palest cream leather upholstery. 'W-what do you want?'

A groan of impatience greeted the tremulous demand.

Tears mingled with the rain on her cheeks. She was glad he couldn't see them. 'G-go away. I'm not going to apologise.'

'I'm offering you a lift home.'

'That's crazy,' she muttered. 'Why w-would you want to do that?'

'Do you think it could possibly be a belated attempt to make amends?'

'No.'

'Oh, Chrissy, how I have missed the delights of dialogue with you. If you don't get in, I'll get out and throw you in. The upholstery's getting wet.'

'I don't w-want a lift!' she gasped. 'You th-think this is funny, don't you?'

'Actually, it's incredibly depressing.' Blaze sighed from the interior. 'If a branch came out to you when you were drowning, you'd push it away and sink like a stone.'

Chrissy was perilously close to another breakdown. 'I h-hate you.'

'And I love you for it, sweetheart. You're unique,' he mocked. 'You see that policeman heading towards us?'

Her head lifted. A uniformed figure was approaching them.

'Stay where you are,' Blaze encouraged. 'This should be fun. He doesn't like the look of us at all. Either you're soliciting or I'm kerb-crawling. The next time we do this, at least run a comb through your hair. At this moment, you're not doing a lot for my image.'

Absorbing the frowning attention they were receiving, Chrissy shot into the car and slammed the door.

'Try not to drip on my CDs.'

She hunched over inelegantly, wet hair screening her pinched profile.

'How is Belle these days?' he enquired, sending the powerful car shooting away from the kerb.

At the reference to her mother, her slight shoulders reared back up, her hair whipping back from her damp cheeks, over-bright eyes raw with pain and condemnation.

'I liked your mother,' Blaze said evenly.

'In so far as you ever noticed her!' Her clogged lashes dropped on her aching eyes. The silence went on and on and on and then she cleared her throat gruffly. 'She's dead.' It was bald, bitter.

'When?'

'Last year.'

'How did it happen?'

She tautened. 'Pneumonia,' she conceded.

'I'm sorry. That must have hurt. You were very close,' he responded with an amount of apparent sincerity that astonished her.

But Chrissy almost laughed out loud. How close had she really been to her mother? Belle Hamilton had fled her husband and family without a word of advance warning. Chrissy had once found her chatting cosily in the kitchen over a cup of coffee with Dennis Carruthers but she hadn't thought anything of it. Belle had always happily offered hospitality to workmen, tradesmen—indeed virtually anyone ordinary who entered the house. She had been far happier entertaining them than she had ever been trying to entertain their grandiose neighbours. Nobody had known about Dennis until it was too late. Her mother had burnt her boats with a vengeance.

'Why didn't you go home again?'

Chrissy turned even paler. 'I couldn't.' And then she regretted even saying that much. But there was something so dangerously unreal about being in Blaze Kenyon's company, something so disturbingly hypnotic about receiving his full attention.

'Where do you live?'

Still in a daze, she told him and then suggested he drop her at a bus-stop. His mouth hardening, he ignored the invitation. From below feathery lashes, she stole a glance at him. He really was quite spectacular. Even immune as she was to his physical allure, she could not resist the urge to look again. Every chiselled line of that strong bone-structure spoke of bred-in-the-bone self-assurance. What could he possibly know about the traumas that had finally torn her family apart when she was sixteen?

Chrissy had stood on the sidelines of her parents' crumbling marriage, helpless to do anything more than offer her unhappy mother sympathy. Her father had been the reasonably contented owner of a hamburger take-away when he won the pools. Overnight their lives had changed out of all recognition. And not for the better. Initially her father's ambitions had been sensible, even modest. He had expanded in the catering trade. But, in the grip of entrepreneurial fever, his ambitions had grown as fast as his bank balance.

When the thrill of flaunting his riches before relatives and friends had worn off, he had bought a fancy house in Berkshire without even consulting her mother. Divided from lifelong friends, her mother had been lost. Worse, Jim Hamilton, always a domineering, short-tempered man, had become more and more aggressive as his wealth and importance grew. When their new and more far-flung neighbours had demonstrated a dismaying reluctance to welcome the Hamiltons into their select social circles, Belle had received the blame.

Even when the locals had finally drifted in to gape, if not to admire, the gulf between her parents had been insurmountable. The damage had been done. Treated with complete contempt by her husband and two eldest children, Belle had been an easy mark for a smooth-tongued younger man. In striking out to find happiness with Dennis, her mother had made an appalling error of judgement. But Chrissy believed that Belle had been driven, not least by her husband's blatant infidelity, into making that final choice.

'I *thought* most of this area was up for redevelopment,' Blaze mused. 'The demolition squad is practically parked on your doorstep.'

It was a dirty little street of narrow terraces, set on the edge of a gigantic building site. Some of the houses were already boarded up.

'Not quite Buck House, is it?' Chrissy snapped in an artificially correct voice, calculated to annoy.

Blaze filtered the car to a smooth halt, carefully avoiding the spill of rubbish from a tumbled dustbin. 'What a little snob you are,' he murmured drily. 'I was only initiating conversation.'

Opening the door with desperate fingers, Chrissy flung him a look of incredulity. 'N-no, you weren't. You can't open your mouth without being superior!'

Without a further word, she skidded out on to the pavement. Rifling in her bag for her key, she hurried down the street to an end terrace and unlocked the door.

'Is that you, Miss Hamilton?'

Swallowing convulsively, Chrissy stilled in the act of closing the door. Her landlady was barring her passage to the stairs. 'You're back early.'

'If you'll excuse me, Mrs Davis——'

'What about the rent? You got it yet?' the older woman interrupted bluntly. 'Because if you haven't you can get out of here today. Give me that key!'

'Mrs Davis, you will get——'

'Nothing ever seems to come of your promises, luv. I must've been mad to take you in. Girls with kiddies in tow aren't reliable. I should have known better,' Mrs Davis fumed. 'But I felt sorry for you, didn't I? Well, I've got my own bills to think about and——'

A crisp, cool voice intervened. 'How much does Miss Hamilton owe you?'

Her landlady spun in amazement. Chalk-pale with mortification and shock, Chrissy's head twisted on her shoulders. Blaze stood in the doorway, not one whit perturbed by the scene he had interrupted. He was pulling a wallet from his jacket.

'Three weeks, she owes,' Mrs Davis retorted truculently, and added the amount.

A handful of notes changed hands faster than Chrissy could part her lips. 'You can't take *his* m-money!' she protested.

'Oh, can't I? I don't care who pays as long as it's paid.' Mrs Davis directed a grim smile of approval at

Blaze. 'And don't you forget that you're to be out of here by Saturday. I've got a removal van booked for the morning.'

Chrissy was so profoundly embarrassed as her landlady disappeared back into her ground-floor flat that she couldn't bring herself even to look at Blaze. 'I'll post it to you,' she promised shakily. 'W-when I can,' honesty bade her admit.

'No hurry.'

She was quite nauseated by the knowledge that she was now in his debt. But she could do nothing but accept his charity. Mrs Davis wouldn't give up the money and Chrissy was in no position to offer repayment. On the other hand, it was thanks to Blaze that she was not now being thrown out on the street. It took immense courage to rise above her sense of humiliation. Raising her bowed head, Chrissy collided with impenetrable sapphire eyes in one brief, stricken connection. 'Thanks,' she forced out with difficulty. 'Maybe I'll see you around some time,' she concluded with awkward finality.

Without awaiting any further response, she started up the stairs, fast. On the first landing, she pressed open the door of her bed-sit with raw relief. She simply couldn't have borne another second of his company.

'What on earth are you doing back?' her babysitter, Karen, demanded, rising from the single armchair with a frown.

'It's a long story.'

Rosie threw herself at Chrissy's knees with a whoop of delight.

'Bloody hell!' a very male voice ejaculated.

Chrissy spun as though she had been jabbed in the back by a hot poker. She hadn't heard Blaze follow her upstairs. He had to move like a leopard on the prowl. With Rosie planting an enthusiastic kiss on her cheek, she was paralysed to the spot, devastatingly conscious of Blaze's stunned and silent scrutiny.

CHAPTER TWO

THERE was a horrible hiatus. Karen hovered the way impressionable females usually did in Blaze's vicinity. Possibly she recognised him. Rarely out of the society pages and the gossip columns, Blaze was very well-known. His life in the fast lane was notorious.

'I'll see you later, Karen,' Chrissy said hurriedly.

As the other girl left with visible reluctance, Blaze strolled deeper into the room, scanning the sparse, worn furniture and the few shabby toys littering the cramped floor space. With a grace of movement that was inbred, he swung back to look at Chrissy, a wry twist to his expressive mouth. 'I suppose I should have been prepared for this scenario,' he drawled. 'But I wasn't. I was still thinking of you as a kid.'

'I'm almost twenty-one.' As she spoke, Rosie was struggling to get down, and reluctantly she bent to lower the wriggling toddler to the floor. She was praying that Blaze would leave, couldn't imagine what strange quirk had made him follow her upstairs.

'Still practically jailbait,' he mused half under his breath.

Her cheeks fired scarlet, her mouth tightening. Did he automatically divide all women into two camps? Those he could sleep with and those he thought he shouldn't sleep with? The idea revolted her, but it also resurrected cringing recollections of their last encounter. Hurriedly, she buried her mind's urge to relive the past. In preference she reflected grimly on Blaze's 'love them and leave them' reputation.

He was an unashamed user and abuser of the female sex, she thought in disgust. Once she had believed that her sister, Elaine, was too calculating to be hurt by any man. But Elaine had fallen hard for Blaze. After a brief whirl, he had ditched her again with savage unconcern, devastating her pride and driving her into a face-saving marriage with a man she didn't love. Her over-confident sister had become just another line in a gossip column, another notch on his bedpost, and for the first time in her life Chrissy had felt sympathy for Elaine.

'So this is the reason you can't go home.' Astonishingly, Blaze crouched down on Rosie's level and solemnly accepted the scruffy pink rabbit he was being invited to admire.

'Wosee's wabbit,' Rosie told him importantly.

'I love wabbits,' Blaze teased, the most natural, utterly breathtaking smile warming his darkly tanned features. The usual chill and cynicism etched there was briefly put to flight. As he ruffled Rosie's black curls, he straightened again.

Bemused by this totally unexpected display of humanity, Chrissy dragged disobedient eyes from the wide, blatantly sensual arc of his mouth. Her chest felt oddly tight as she sucked in oxygen, suddenly short of breath.

Blaze sighed. 'It's probably a very stupid question, but how the hell did you land yourself in a mess like this?'

He had simply assumed that Rosie was *her* child. But then, everybody did. In the circumstances it was a natural assumption, and she could not possibly trust him with the truth. Rosie was her half-sister, the last pathetic footnote to her late mother's 'marriage' to Dennis Carruthers.

'I think you should leave,' she said stiffly.

'You're right. I should walk back out of here and forget I ever left the car,' Blaze murmured grimly. 'But I have the hideous suspicion that all this would travel with me. Clearly you're broke, and now you're also unemployed——'

'And whose f-fault is that?' she cut in shrilly.

'I'm not in the habit of censoring speech in private conversation,' he countered without an ounce of embarrassment. 'But if I said one thing that was unfounded on fact, you're welcome to call me to account over it.'

The invitation merely made her turn away in sharp distress. Dear God, how she loathed him! But he had uttered not a single untruth. The bald facts were exactly as he had stated them. *Nouveau riche* and painfully rough round the edges, the Hamiltons had certainly failed to merge tastefully with the surrounding countryside. Her father had loved putting on vulgar displays of his new-found wealth. He had thought that he needed to impress people to win respect. But all that he had won was derision.

'I gather that you have to get out of here,' Blaze prompted shortly. 'Have you found somewhere else to go?'

'No.' The admission was dredged from her. Not that he needed it. He would know as well as she did that she had no hope of finding somewhere else without cold, hard cash to put down in advance.

London was a terrifyingly anonymous place to live in without friends. Those Chrissy had made at college had swiftly drifted away when she was forced to drop out of her teacher-training course and shoulder full-time care and responsibility for her little sister. In one gigantic bound, Chrissy had gone from teenage freedom to adult reality. She had grown up ten years in the first six months.

A succinct and unsuppressed swear word fell from his lips. 'What are you planning to do this weekend?' he demanded harshly. 'Set up home on the street?'

'We'll manage,' she muttered tightly.

'Like you're managing now?' he derided cruelly. 'Have you asked your father for help?'

'I haven't spoken to him in three years,' she confided unsteadily. 'He was f-furious when I moved in with Mum down here. He doesn't know about Rosie and it wouldn't make any difference if he did. As far as he's concerned, I betrayed him when I went to Mum——'

'Your brother? Your sister?' Blaze cut in. 'Surely one of them——?'

Chrissy vented a humourless laugh at the ridiculous idea of either Rory or Elaine taking up the cudgels on their behalf or even putting their hands into their pockets. Rory lived in California now with his wife and family and, just like Elaine, he had been appalled by what their mother had done. Neither had been willing to forgive Belle. Even when she was lying in Intensive Care, her life expectancy measured in hours, Elaine had refused Chrissy's pleas for her to come down to London.

Chrissy had never got the chance to tell them about Rosie and, in any case, the revelation would only provoke horror and disgust. Rosie was Belle's daughter by another man, the result of an illegal union that had made headlines for days in the tabloids when Dennis was arrested. After all, Belle hadn't been the only woman he had deceived into a quick trip to the altar. There had been two others, neither of whom he had bothered to divorce.

'I never got on that well with Dad anyway,' Chrissy pointed out, eager to close the subject because she didn't want to tell lies.

'Who would?' Blaze breathed with chilling hauteur. 'He'd sell his granny to cannibals to make a fast buck.'

As he made the grim assurance, cold, clear anger lightened his eyes and tautened his sculpted cheekbones. Chrissy stared, puzzled by his vehemence. What had her father done to rouse his ire? But before she could voice her curiosity Blaze shrugged back a silk shirt-cuff and glanced at his watch. 'I've got a business meeting in an hour.'

'I'll post that money to you,' she said again.

'Forget it,' he advised carelessly. 'Consider it small compensation for the loss of your job.'

A painful flush stained her pallor. 'I don't want your ch-charity!'

'Think of it as conscience money.' Narrowed very blue eyes lingered on the betraying shimmer of tears below her lashes, the defeat slumping her shoulders. 'I owe you and right now you need a helping hand,' he intoned with a faintly scornful twist of his mouth as if he couldn't quite credit how anyone of intelligence could end up in such a situation.

'I don't w-want your helping hand! I don't want your lousy money!' Chrissy spat.

'I'm afraid you're stuck with it,' Blaze informed her flatly. 'If it's not too rude a question ... where's Rosie's father?'

'Behind bars!' Chrissy told him fiercely.

'In prison?' She really had his attention now. For a split-second, he actually looked shocked. Blaze, the un-shockable, shocked. Lush black lashes, inherited along with his golden skin tone from his Spanish father, briefly veiled his astonishingly noticeable eyes from her view. 'When you screw up, you go the full yard, don't you?' he murmured.

She couldn't quite believe her ears, and then she re-membered that this was Blaze, who followed few of the rules that governed other people's behaviour. He was prone to saying exactly what he thought with a brand of devastating honesty that frequently unnerved those around him. He had no time for civilised dissimulation. His raw energy always had an edge of impatience, as if restlessness ran in his bloodstream.

'I want you to go,' she said.

He studied her with grim detachment. She was at the end of her rope. He knew it, and she hated him for it. 'Either you go home and crawl or you fling yourself on the tender mercies of the social services,' he drawled. 'You can't make it without somebody's help——'

'Will you get out of here?' Chrissy wrenched open the door with violence. She was shaking with the force of her emotions.

For a split-second, Blaze stilled. He stared down into her blazing green eyes, and for the first time that day they really connected. She fell into bottomless blue like a novice swimmer and forgot to breathe, her throat tightening, an electrifying tension shooting through her slim body.

He ran a blunt forefinger along the ripe fullness of her soft lower lip, and his touch was a flame dancing provocation on her too sensitive skin. 'You are extraordinarily intense. You feel, you really do feel. That's bound to get you into tight corners. Intensity is a passport to pain. Don't you know that yet?'

Burnt by that near caress and his proximity, she leapt back, staggered and dazed by the sensations she had briefly experienced. If it was at all possible, her hatred intensified to the brink of explosion. His pity blistered into her skin like acid. 'Go on, g-get out!' she practically screamed at him.

When he had gone, the room was strangely shrunken in its emptiness. She blinked, shook her head uncertainly, and shivered. Once before he had made her feel like that. Trapped, hypnotised, lost. It was petrifying, overwhelming. Self could not seem to exist when he came too close. But this time, at least, he hadn't lost his temper.

Few were aware of it, but a seething black temper lurked behind those stunningly blue eyes and that cool half-smile. Once, just once, she had fallen foul of that temper by accidentally stumbling into the firing line. But he clearly didn't remember that...oh, no, why should he? It was only little Chrissy he had bitten to the bone with that cruel whiplash tongue, only little Chrissy, offspring of the infamously vulgar Hamilton clan. Why should he remember half frightening her out of her wits?

She was dismayed by the emotion shuddering through her in great waves, could hardly believe that she could still feel so strongly after all this time. Yet she did. Once he had touched her with raw sexual derision, just once, when she was seventeen and stupidly, recklessly naïve. It had been over in seconds but she had never forgotten the humiliation of his drunken assumption that she was throwing herself at his head as so many other women had.

Nor had she forgotten the resounding force of his savage rejection. Without ever issuing the smallest invitation to him, she had been flung away, thrust bodily out of reach as if she was too utterly revolting to be borne. Reeling with shame and confusion at what he had made her feel, she had then been forced to withstand a verbal beating into the bargain.

'If you don't watch out, you'll turn into a tart like that sister of yours!' Blaze had intoned viciously. 'I may have been a few times round the block but I do have some standards!'

Nor had the brutality ended there on that unforgivable insult to Elaine. With an explicit lack of inhibition, Blaze had told her what he thought of her and what would happen if she continued on the promiscuous path he had so ridiculously imagined her to be embarking on. If anything, the moral lecture from his immoral corner had been salt rubbed into the wound.

That he could have thought even for a conceited moment that she *wanted* him...that she was just another bimbo willing to do absolutely anything to get him. The recollection still made her feel sick. She had not had a teenage crush on Blaze Kenyon. She had never, ever denied that physically he was almost unbelievably attractive. But she had never been able to stand him. As a human being he scored nil all the way down the line. Like a chalk scraping down a blackboard, he set her teeth on edge.

Yet the split-second savagery of his mouth on hers had devastated her. She had felt her own response with disbelief and horror. The shame of that momentary self-betrayal had been agonising. And, linked with his derision, the agony had become anguish. He might as well have stripped her naked and tossed her into a crowded street to be laughed at. Endowed with all the sensitivity he lacked, Chrissy had felt suicidal.

'So what next?' Karen grimaced, shrugging into her coat and hauling her suitcase on to the landing. 'You worry me to death.'

'If I go to the social services,' Chrissy whispered tautly, 'they'll probably put Rosie in care.'

'Stuff!' Karen said. 'They'll stick you in a hostel or a B and B.'

'I don't have any right to keep her,' Chrissy reminded her painfully. 'And if they ask Dennis what he wants, he's sure to say adoption. He never wanted her in the first place.'

'What's it got to do with him?' Karen snorted.

'He is her father. He's got more rights than I've got...'

'She's a sweet kid, but I don't know why you want to be lumbered at your age,' the older girl admitted bluntly. 'I mean, she really isn't your responsibility. And let's face it, kiddo...what can you give her?'

'Karen!' Chrissy was shaken and hurt by that forthright assessment.

'Look, this isn't easy to say, but adoption would give her a good home and two parents. Be practical, Chrissy.' Karen sighed ruefully. 'I can't cut it here without a job. That's why I'm going back to Liverpool. How do you expect to make it with a child?'

'Other people do!'

'They have to. You don't. Rosie does have other options,' Karen stressed. 'You have to face facts some time. Even if you do get another job, you won't make enough to cover childcare. You just haven't got the earning power.'

It was a relief when Karen's cab arrived. Like it or not, the other woman had faced her with certain inescapable facts. Karen had looked after Rosie for a pittance and the arrangement had only been temporary. Sooner or later, Chrissy would have been faced with finding a replacement, and her salary would not have stretched to the going rate. Not if she had wanted them to eat as well.

But Karen also made her see something that she had refused to see before. Was she being selfish in her desire to keep Rosie? Rosie didn't have enough clothes or toys or stimulation. All those things cost money they didn't have. Perhaps worst of all was the acknowledgement that she couldn't even give her sister security. She didn't even know where they'd be sleeping in forty-eight hours' time. What sort of life was that to give Rosie? Didn't she deserve more?

Chrissy was afraid of approaching the social services. She was not Rosie's legal guardian. Apart from the registration of her birth, the authorities had had no further notice of her sister's existence. They had moved three times while Belle was still alive, on each occasion to smaller, cheaper apartments. Her mother, stubbornly set on denying Rosie's existence, had refused to take up her entitlement to child benefit. The very frequency of their changes of address had put paid to any further enquiries from the powers-that-be.

So far they had fallen through the system . . . but what would happen if they were forced to seek help? Would she lose Rosie? That fear had prevented Chrissy from attempting to put her relationship with her baby sister on a proper legal footing. Furthermore, as she had told Karen, Dennis would be sure to be asked what he wanted, and Dennis, who had been furious when her mother became pregnant, would be certain to opt for adoption.

Chrissy didn't believe that she could love a child of her own body more than she loved Rosie. Belle had never come to terms with what Dennis had done to her. It was the pregnancy which had killed Belle. Not so much the strain of carrying a baby at the age of forty-five as the shame of all that had gone before. Dennis's rejection when he'd realised that her mother was running out of money. His arrest, the publicity. The horrific sense of humiliation with which Belle had endured her pregnancy.

After the birth, Chrissy had hoped that her mother would recover. But she hadn't. Sinking deeper and deeper into depression, Belle had lost all pride in her appearance and had done the barest minimum necessary in caring for Rosie. She had refused to see a doctor. In desperation, Chrissy had approached the doctor herself, begging him to visit. Unfortunately, Belle had put on a terrific act for his benefit, and after his departure there had been the most terrible row and Belle had threatened to throw Chrissy out if she ever interfered again.

Inevitably her mother had neglected her own health, and chest problems that had troubled her in earlier years had returned. A bout of flu had turned into pneumonia. She had been rushed into hospital but it had been too late.

Belle had had no will to fight for survival. She had simply drifted away. At the time of her death, they had been on the brink of moving again, and after the funeral Chrissy had gone ahead with the move. Only the doctor had enquired about Rosie's welfare, and Chrissy had lied. She had told him that she would take her sister home to her family and, not knowing the circumstances of Rosie's birth, he had not questioned that story.

At half-eight the next morning, a loud knock landed on the door. Opening it a crack, Chrissy's troubled eyes focused incredulously on Blaze Kenyon. Taking advantage of her bemusement, he pressed the door wide and strolled in.

'Have you had breakfast yet?'

'Breakfast?' she echoed foolishly.

'I didn't want to miss you. That's why I came early.' He hunkered down on his knees to respond to Rosie's rush in his direction. 'Friendly little scrap, isn't she? Have you got a sitter for her?'

'No.' In a complete daze, Chrissy stared at him, wincing as her little sister flung herself at him with gay abandon. 'Friendly' was an understatement. Rosie was all over him like a rash. Men were almost non-existent in her world. Blaze was an object of curiosity.

'Carry... carry Wosee,' she demanded.

'Hold on a minute,' Blaze drawled as he dug a mobile phone out of the holster on his belt. Calmly holding it out of Rosie's reach, he punched out a number and ordered a cab to their address.

'W-why do you want a cab?' Chrissy enquired.

Blaze swung Rosie into his arms and vaulted upright again. 'There's no room for a child in my car.'

Chrissy folded her arms. 'But we're not going anywhere.'

'I'm taking you out to breakfast. Does the scrap need a bottle or something?' He surveyed Rosie uncertainly.

'She's nearly two and a half,' Chrissy said drily.

A broad shoulder sheathed in a black cashmere sweater moved in a careless shrug. 'Children are a closed book to me.'

Maybe he thought they were in need of a good square meal. She couldn't think of any other explanation for his arrival. Her cheeks flaming, she said, 'Look, we're not going anywhere. We don't need breakfast——'

'You're so thin you look anorexic. You're not, are you?' he prompted with a sudden frown.

'Of course I'm n-not,' she snapped in frustration.

A mocking grin slanted his mouth. 'I couldn't cope with an anorexic. I'm crazy about food.'

It didn't show anywhere on that long, lean body. He didn't carry an ounce of surplus flesh. His black jeans hugged sleek thighs and narrow hips, his sweater delineating a muscular chest and a stomach as flat as a washboard. About there she dragged her gaze away from him, angry with herself.

Blaze, at Rosie's prompting, was obediently retrieving her rabbit from the floor and receiving a beatific smile in reward. Chrissy couldn't quite believe what she was seeing. There was no sign of irritation or impatience in his dark, mobile features.

'I've got a job offer for you,' he told her almost in an aside.

Chrissy tensed like a greyhound scenting a hare. 'Where? Who with?' she demanded.

'I talk better on a full stomach. Don't get excited,' he warned. 'It's not in London and it might not appeal to you.'

So this was why he was here. His conscience had pushed him into further effort on their behalf. She reddened fiercely. It was petty of her but he was the last male in the world she wanted help from. It smacked too much of *noblesse oblige* and stung her pride. But then what was pride when it came to Rosie? And why was she getting excited? She might not get the job whatever it was and, even if she did, where would they live and what about Rosie? One problem simply led to another.

In the cab, Rosie stayed anchored to Blaze. She sat there very solemn and quiet and on her very best behaviour, but no way would she return to Chrissy.

'No... no want Kissy,' she said quite clearly.

'Kissy?' Blaze cast Chrissy a sudden lancing look of derision. 'She's not Kissy. She's Mummy,' he informed Rosie firmly. 'Mummy. Say it.'

Rosie obliged.

'What the heck do you th-think you're doing?' Chrissy spat at him furiously.

'I've got no time for women who won't let their children call them Mother——'

'It's nothing to do with you!' Chrissy vented in an explosive response. 'How dare you interfere——?'

'I know exactly what I'm talking about.' He was quite unrepentant. 'She needs to know who you are.'

Chrissy bit down on her tongue. She was angry, but did it matter? After today, she was unlikely to see him again, and Rosie would soon forget. Since she couldn't trust him with the truth, she would keep quiet.

He took them to a really fancy hotel where the head waiter treated them to an incredible amount of personal attention. As soon as Rosie was settled, Chrissy unleashed her impatience. 'The job,' she reminded him.

'Live-in. Child not objected to. It's a big house,' he volunteered, lounging back in his chair to regard her with clear, cool eyes. 'One permanent occupant, occasional guests.'

Her brow furrowed. This she had not expected. 'A private house?'

He nodded.

'Where?'

'Your home stomping grounds.'

Chrissy tautened in dismay. That was equally unexpected. 'How close?'

'About five miles from Southfork.'

Chrissy reddened. Her father had christened his home The Towers. It hadn't really matched up with the Spanish arches and the lamp-posts lining the drive. The locals had gone one better.

'What's the job?' she asked anxiously, striving not to think of what it would be like to be working so close to her own home.

Blaze was tucking into an enormous fry-up with gusto. There was silence for several minutes. She could have screamed. He had her hanging on his every word. Finally, he let his knife and fork rest and lifted his coffee instead. 'Cook...housekeeper...general maid of all work. I've got to be honest. The job description would have to be fairly elastic. If you can't be flexible, it won't suit you.'

'Are you telling me that I'm likely to be worked to death?'

'No. Other staff will be brought in if it's necessary. Right now, there's no need for them,' he asserted. 'The house is being extensively renovated. It's in one hell of a mess and mostly unfurnished. The owner hasn't moved in yet and you would be left to your own devices quite a lot. There is a phone, though, and the use of a car. So what do you think?'

'Any idea of the salary?'

He came back with a very generous quote. 'Not a lot, I know, but you wouldn't have any bills to worry about.'

Chrissy grinned. 'Are you kidding? I'd be in clover.' And then she strove to suppress her excitement and be sensible. It was too good to be true. There had to be more drawbacks than he had mentioned. 'Why am I getting a chance?'

'Someone else backed out at the last minute. Took one look at the state of the house and said, "No way",' Blaze revealed.

'I have no references——'

'If you can cook worth a damn, you're in,' he assured her.

She bit her lip. 'What's he like...? The owner, I mean.'

Blaze lazed back in his seat with a reflective air. A satiric brow elevated. 'He's not likely to come creeping into your bed in the middle of the night, if that's what you mean——'

'Th-that thought hadn't even occurred to me!'

He raked grimly amused eyes over her pink cheeks. 'He does have a sex life, though.'

Chrissy studied her plate. 'H-hardly anything to do with me.'

'He likes a quiet life in every other way. Prefers horses to people, spends most of his time outdoors. He's not fussy about his surroundings. You won't be expected to polish the furniture to a mirror shine——'

'If he gets married all that will change,' she mused absently.

'He'll never get married,' Blaze countered with a sardonic smile. 'No reason to, every reason not to.'

'How soon could I get an interview?' Chrissy pressed.

'You've just had it,' Blaze told her carelessly, his attention switching to Rosie, who was striving hopelessly to stretch a short arm far enough from her high-chair to filch a mushroom off his plate.

'Stop that, Rosie. You can't have it,' Chrissy admonished by rote. 'Are you saying that I can have the job on your recommendation?' she said, turning back to Blaze.

Rosie got her mushroom.

'If you want it, it's yours.'

'He must be a very good friend.' As bait, it failed, drawing no response. Sensing that Blaze was becoming bored with the subject, Chrissy asked, 'How soon could I start?'

'As soon as you can get yourself up there.'

Rosie was now casting languishing looks at the fried tomato.

Blaze surrendered and cast Chrissy a look of reproof. 'You should have let me order her a proper meal. She's starving!'

'She just likes eating off other people's plates.' She watched him sipping his coffee, the cup cradled elegantly in one lean hand.

If this job panned out, she would probably see him again. Torbald Manor, his late grandfather's home, would only be about ten miles away. Did he still live there? Her brow furrowed. She wasn't very well up on the rules of aristocratic inheritance. The title, she was aware, had gone to his uncle, and even if Blaze had been next in line, it couldn't have gone to him. His mother had never married his father.

'He's illegitimate!' Elaine had gasped when she found out. 'Would you believe it...? I mean, in a family like *that*!'

'Are you finished?' Blaze regarded her expectantly.

'Yes.' She pushed away her cup as though she had finished. She could feel his impatience.

'I have to be in Brighton by noon.'

In the cab, he got a call on his mobile phone. Something about a horse-box and an accident. His language was choice. Chrissy wanted to cover Rosie's ears. She sent him a dirty look but he was too intent on the call to notice. The cab dropped them off seconds before he completed the call.

Sending a fleeting glance at his watch, he breathed, 'Transport...that's a bit of a problem...'

'Transport?' she repeated uncertainly.

'Can you catch the train to Reading?'

She nodded.

'Right, make it tomorrow afternoon, OK?' He unlocked his car, reached in for a notepad and scribbled something down on it. 'Call that number when you arrive and someone will come and pick you up. Ask for the head lad——'

'The head what?'

'Ask for Hamish,' he rephrased tersely. 'He'll ferry you back to the Hall.'

Ten seconds later he was in the driver's seat. Ten after that, he was gone. Rosie's bottom lip wobbled alarmingly. They had been dumped without ceremony.

Mrs Davis was hovering in the hallway, quite an achievement in so cramped a space. 'You seem to have solved your problems,' she said archly.

'Sorry, I——'

'Don't think I don't know who he is. Well...well...well, I thought to myself last night,' she confided. '"Fancy it being him," I said to my Stan. He's decided to meet his obligations, has he? Not before time——'

'I don't know what you're talking about.' Chrissy was trying to edge past the older woman.

Mrs Davis pursed her lips, her sudden congeniality waning at the lack of feedback. 'He doesn't want anyone to know, does he? But anyone with eyes in their head could tell she was his kid. Same hair, same eyes. You should have sold your story to a newspaper. They pay a lot for that sort of stuff...'

As the penny dropped, Chrissy's jaw dropped with it. She was implying that Rosie was Blaze's child. 'Of course she's n-not his,' she stammered in horror. 'She's got absolutely n-nothing to do with him!'

Mrs Davis stepped back but she had the last word. 'But he pays your rent when he has to,' she said with a smirk.

Just because Rosie had black hair and blue eyes! On such slender possibilities to assume... The cheek of the woman! Clearly she spent too much time reading the murkier tabloids. However, Mrs Davis didn't have the power to hold Chrissy's thoughts for very long.

She swept Rosie up into an exuberant hug. 'We've got a job, Rosie! Use of a car, did you hear that bit? This man is going to eat as if he's staying at the Ritz,' she swore feelingly. 'Whatever it takes, we'll stick it out.'

'This man', she repeated to herself. For goodness' sake, Blaze hadn't even given her his name! 'The Hall', he had said. Her brow furrowed. It didn't ring any bells of recognition, yet she would have believed that she knew every sizeable house within a ten-mile radius of her former home.

'I'm sorry that we were so late,' Chrissy said again, hoping to lighten the atmosphere.

'Aye,' Hamish responded dourly and that appeared to be the height of his conversational ability since she had got little else from him since he'd picked them up in a Land Rover at the station. A bomb scare had thrown the trains into chaos. They had been lucky to get on a train at all. But the explanation hadn't cut much ice with Hamish.

He was a wiry little Scotsman with the build of an ex-jockey. He had taken one look at her and Rosie and his astonishment had been palpable. Evidently they weren't what he had expected. She had seen him squinting at her naked wedding-ring finger, watched his weather-beaten face go tight with disapproval. The chill in the air was not her imagination.

Chrissy's nerves were starting to respond to that chill. What if Blaze had taken too much upon himself in hiring her? What if Hamish's boss was as taken aback by the sight of them as Hamish had been? Rosie was asleep under her arm, a dead weight of toddler exhaustion. Chrissy didn't feel much livelier. All she wanted was a bed for the night. Tomorrow she would worry herself to death about the future, not tonight.

The headlights illuminated trees and hedgerows and little else, but she knew exactly where they were even if she didn't know where they were going to end up. Then Hamish turned off the road into the village and up a long, steep lane. In her time, it had been overgrown and pot-holed. Now it was trimmed and surfaced.

'Mrs Easton's house!' she exclaimed involuntarily.

'Westleigh Hall,' Hamish corrected.

'But I thought it was derelict.' Chrissy had never seen the house because it was so far from the road, but she did recall the old lady in the funny hats in church. She had died and the house had lain empty ever since.

'Practically. The guv'nor's got vision.' Hamish looked as if he might actually have said more, and then he glanced at her and compressed his lips.

They drove past a brightly lit lodge. The Hall was a grey stone edifice, built on irregular lines. That was all she saw in the flare of the headlights because it was in complete darkness.

Hamish took her cases and Chrissy struggled out with Rosie, trying not to wake her. The front door wasn't locked. He reached for a light switch and then muttered, 'Electric must still be off.'

'You're kidding me,' Chrissy groaned.

He disappeared and she heard him banging about through cupboards. He returned with a torch and showed her into a vast, cheerless kitchen. 'There should be some food in the fridge. I'll be leaving you, then,' he said.

And he did. She sank down on a chair with Rosie. She wanted to put her head down and cry. There was no heat, no light. Well, what did you expect, Chrissy? she asked herself. You're not a guest, entitled to expect a three-star welcome. You're the housekeeper. Rising upright, she settled Rosie into a huddle on a sagging armchair. She covered her with her coat and prayed that she would stay asleep while she searched out a bed for them both.

Climbing those stairs was the creepiest experience Chrissy had ever had. The torchlight cast weird leaping shadows and accentuated dark, forbidding doorways. She shone it into room after room and discovered three sparkling new bathrooms, but there appeared to be only one furnished bedroom.

At the end of the huge landing, a corridor ran off unexpectedly to the left and a narrow flight of stairs disappeared up into the gloom of the attics. At least, she assumed they led to the attics, for her explorations had been forced to a halt by an untidy stack of floorboards. Between her and the remainder of the upper floor stretched a ten-foot-wide chasm of bare joists.

The discovery gave Chrissy quite a start. Just suppose that she hadn't been looking where she was going? Blaze hadn't been joking when he'd said that the house was in a state. And presumably the one furnished bedroom was for her.

She lugged up the cases, scanned the room with a sigh and then hauled a battered *chaise-longue* over to the side of the king-size divan. Opening up their luggage, she made up a bed for Rosie on the *chaise-longue*. Rosie, who twisted and turned all night long, was murder to share a bed with.

Downstairs the fridge revealed three bottles of champagne, a wizened tomato and an abandoned lunchbox with mouldy contents. She found biscuits in a cupboard but what she really wanted was a decent cup of tea.

Unfortunately the ancient range in one corner was stone-cold. Her mouth tightening expressively, Chrissy surrendered. It was obvious that nobody gave two hoots about her comfort! Lifting Rosie, she carried her upstairs. At least if she went to bed she would be warm.

Naturally there was no hot water in the nearest bathroom. It didn't surprise her. Shivering with cold, she checked on her sister, cosily snuggled up beneath her blankets, and then she doused the torch and dived into the chilly embrace of the bed. She slept instantly, felled at last by the traumas of the past week.

But once she started having the dream—that dream unlike any other in her experience—it seemed so real that she briefly thought she was awake. Where once she had been cold, she was hot in the grip of an amazingly erotic fantasy where she lay in a shameless tangle of limbs.

It wasn't she lying there while male hands roamed slowly, expertly over every quivering inch of flesh tantalisingly shielded by a thin layer of cotton. It wasn't she who arched and moaned when knowing fingers skimmed over the straining mounds of her breasts, her nipples tightening instantly into an almost painful sensitivity. And most certainly it wasn't she who dragged him hungrily down to her in the darkness and virtually crashed into combustible collision with the hot, hard urgency of his devouring mouth.

The surge of excitement that engulfed her was reassuringly *unreal*. She was a burning current, a blazing fuse wire hurtling at a breakneck pace towards dynamite, nothing on her mind but the terrible need for that imminent explosion. And then somewhere in the darkness there came a tiny recognisable sound, a faint gurgle as Rosie mumbled in her sleep, a sound so inherently familiar that Chrissy's eyes shot wide open and then she knew she was awake. Oh, lord, did she know, still trapped beneath the demanding weight of an all-male body.

Tearing her swollen mouth free, she jerked her head away with a rising moan of horror. 'Get off me!' she gasped, stricken.

Two things happened almost simultaneously. Suddenly she was free. Suddenly the air was blue with male outrage. No awakening could have been more violent or terrifying. Sixth sense told her who had been taking advantage of her virtually inanimate body while she had believed she was dreaming. But sixth sense was choosing an identity almost more threatening than that of a total stranger, so she refused to listen to it.

A lamp went on, illuminating the scene. Sitting bolt upright, clutching the duvet to her like a protective cocoon, Chrissy was shattered into complete silence by the sight that met her frightened gaze.

'What the hell are you doing in my bed?' Blaze raked at her from between gritted teeth.

CHAPTER THREE

CHRISSY took one glazed look at him and then closed her eyes. 'D-don't you think you ought to put some clothes on?'

'I want an explanation!' Blaze grated as though he were the one with the grounds for most complaint.

She could still see him in her mind's eye. Six feet three inches of lean, all-male virility and not a stitch of clothing to interrupt the view. Embarrassment, bewilderment and incredulity held her in paralysis. What was he doing in this house? What was he doing in the only bed? What, worst of all, had she allowed him to do to her?

'W-will you get out of here?' she spat, lifting her lashes too soon and catching a glimpse of his long golden back view as he hauled up a pair of jeans.

'This is my room!' he roared back at her.

Chrissy was trembling. 'You're going to w-wake Rosie...'

'Rosie?' Aghast, he strode round to her side of the bed and stared down in disbelief at the small curled-up shape showing only a fluff of tousled hair above the blankets. 'She's in here as well? We might've—she might've *seen*—— Bloody hell!'

Without warning, he bent down, scooped Chrissy bodily out of the bed and, striding to the door, he deposited her on the landing. Then, practically on tiptoe and with an exaggerated care which would have been sheer comedy in any other circumstances, he closed the door. He needn't have bothered. Rosie slept like the dead.

'We'll discuss this downstairs,' he bit out fiercely.

'I'd l-like to know w-what you're doing here,' Chrissy dared, shivering with cold and barefoot into the bargain.

41

'Downstairs,' he repeated with arrogant emphasis. 'And the explanation had better be good.'

Ignoring him, Chrissy went back into the bedroom and crossed the floor to where her case lay open. Pulling out an outsize sweater, she donned it in haste.

'If you wake that baby, I'll hit the roof!' he spat like an avenging angel.

'Nothing short of an earthquake wakes her when she's really tired,' Chrissy muttered.

'Am I supposed to be grateful for that?' He took the stairs two at a time.

'W-well, it's more than I've got to be grateful for,' Chrissy shot at him shakily. 'How d-dare you put your filthy hands on me?'

'Hell's teeth,' he seethed. 'I didn't know it was you!'

He strode into the kitchen, illuminating lights all the way.

'I thought the electricity was off,' she breathed irrelevantly.

'Switched off. The builders forgot to put it on again.' Blaze threw himself down on a chair by the scarred kitchen table and fixed smouldering sapphire-blue eyes on her shrinking figure. 'What were you doing in my bed?'

'It's the only bed in the house,' she protested, wondering how on earth he was managing to make *her* feel the one most in the wrong.

'The furniture I had in storage was supposed to arrive this afternoon.' In the long pause, he studied her intently and there was a new, disturbing light in that all-enveloping gaze. 'I didn't check when I came in. I put on the electric, came upstairs and got into bed in the dark. I didn't want to wake you and the kid up by making a lot of noise——'

'Your consideration o-overwhelms me.' Furniture in storage. The truth had been shouting at her from the instant she sat up in that bed. She just hadn't wanted to believe it. 'Th-this is your h-house, isn't it?'

'Yeah, and I'm a lot like Baby Bear when I find someone uninvited in my bed,' he drawled sardonically.

He hadn't denied it. Westleigh Hall belonged to him yet he had hired her without telling her that fact. Indeed he had deliberately deceived her. A deep flush carmined her fine skin. She was so shaken by the realisation that her tongue was glued to the roof of her mouth. This was her employer. Blaze Kenyon. What was he playing at? What was to happen now? Had he offered her the job as a cruel joke?

Dimly she had assumed that her new boss might be a little strapped for cash and that was why he was willing to take on someone without references or any real experience. Blaze's Ferrari put paid to that idea. She found it hard to believe that Blaze had not been able to find someone more suitable... someone without a child in tow.

'I didn't know it was y-your bed... It was the only bed,' she reminded him in an undertone. 'We had to sleep somewhere. There was no light, no food, no heat——'

'Money for food.' With a flourish, Blaze slapped down a handful of notes and a small sheet of paper instructing her to do some shopping. It had been sitting on the top of the fridge, which was taller than she was. With only the aid of a torch, she would never have seen it.

'We only got here at t-ten.' She explained about the bomb scare. 'I didn't see the note.'

'I was expecting food tonight,' he divulged grimly.

Chrissy understood why women occasionally battered men to death. She thought of their joyless arrival and the complete absence of anyone willing to show them how to settle in.

'If the furniture didn't come, Hamish should have taken you back to the lodge to spend the night with him and Floss,' Blaze mused impatiently. 'Weren't you prepared to accept the offer?'

She nearly told him the truth, but that might get the charmless Hamish into trouble. If there was the smallest chance that she could work here...and she couldn't afford not to fight for that chance...it wouldn't be a good idea to get on the wrong side of Blaze's other employees. 'I didn't want to bother them,' she muttered. 'I think he was busy.'

'I pay him to be busy at what I tell him to be busy at.' It was chillingly cold and she suppressed a shiver. 'Why don't you put on the kettle? I could do with something warm...considering that the something that was warming me up appears to be out of bounds.'

'K-kettle?' she echoed jerkily, naïvely unbalanced by that softly added *double entendre*.

'The object with the spout and the flex.'

Mercifully she espied it on the top of the fridge. She filled it although she felt more like throwing it at him. 'W-why didn't you tell me that I'd be working for you?'

'I didn't want you to turn it down without thinking it through,' he murmured flatly. 'You weren't going to get a second chance. I need a housekeeper without a lot of fancy ideas and you need a job. Basically, that's all there was to it.'

But she sensed something more. Biting at her lower lip, she glanced across at him. His shirt hung open, framing the muscular brown breadth of his chest and the curling black hair hazing his pectorals before it arrowed down over his flat stomach. In the act of staring, she caught herself up and shut her eyes on an aching sense of chagrin and confusion. Was she becoming like all the rest? Couldn't she take her eyes off him? Or was it that much harder now since that night all those years ago when he had touched her and the whole world had vanished as though he had pressed a destruct button somewhere deep down inside her?

And if that was true, how did she feel after tonight? She did not feel equal to meeting those fiercely intelligent eyes of his. She might have believed she was

dreaming, but she had responded wildly to those inti-
macies. She had never felt like that before, but then she
hadn't had much opportunity to experiment, she reminded herself. Maybe any experienced male could make
a woman feel like that...but only if the chemistry was
right.

That shook her rigid. How could she continue to deny
that she found him physically attractive? She had melted
in his arms. She had been electrified by his touch. And
if that was so obvious to her, how much more obvious
was it to him? All of a sudden, she knew she couldn't
bear to stay in this house and work for him.

'The kettle's boiling.'

He was so cool now. What had happened in that bed
might almost have existed only in her imagination. 'I
don't think I can stay after——'

He expelled a long, laconic sigh. 'After what? I didn't
know you were there. I turned over and found a female
body and reacted on instinct...'

Chrissy was mortified. 'That's s-so disgusting.'

Blaze raised a winged brow. 'You talk like a teenage
virgin, but you didn't find Rosie under any gooseberry
bush——'

'I don't w-want to talk about it!' In her distress, her
back was rigidly presented to him.

'You must concede that I have some grounds for curiosity. Did you love Rosie's father?'

She spun round. 'No!' she rebutted with sharp distaste and then abruptly she remembered that she was
talking for her mother, not herself. Reddening, she muttered, 'I thought I did but, when it came down to it, it
was j-just an infatuation.'

'Are you in touch with him...?' Unusually he hesitated. 'I mean, do you visit him?'

'No.'

'Are you waiting for him?'

Feeling foolish, she shook her head, refusing to look
at him.

'That would appear to bring us back to what happened between us——'

'Leave it alone!' she broke in fiercely.

'Why should I?' Blaze traded. 'Another few minutes and I'd have had you——'

Chrissy shuddered. 'No!'

With veiled eyes, he surveyed her appearance in the sloppy sweater that did little to conceal the slender length of her perfect legs. Tousled dark hair with brighter streaks the shade of autumn leaves cascaded round her triangular face, highlighting luminous green eyes and a wide, generous mouth. 'You're incredibly sexy,' he breathed in a different tone of voice altogether, an almost predatory purr deepening his vowel sounds.

It was like being touched. With difficulty, she dredged her stunned scrutiny from him and doggedly asked, 'D-do you take milk and sugar?'

There was a pin-dropping silence. She pretended not to notice it. He hadn't meant what he had said; of course he hadn't. It was just that certain dangerous boundaries had been breached between them. It was just that it was second nature to him to lapse into that incredibly physical intensity with a woman. Or maybe, having sunk low enough to touch her, even half asleep, he felt he had to justify that intimacy by exaggerating her attractions. Whatever, if she ignored it, it would go away, and sooner or later she would stop squirming with embarrassment.

'Blaze...' she had to prompt shakily

'One sugar, no milk.'

The raw tension visible in her slim shoulders eased. She set a cup and saucer down about a foot from him.

'I only bite after midnight on request,' he said softly. 'Join me.'

It wasn't an invitation, it was a command. She tensed and it really sunk in then that she was utterly dependent on his goodwill. In a series of stiff movements, she made herself a coffee and sat down awkwardly at the table with him.

'You don't like me. Relax,' he urged as her head jerked up in dismay. 'It really doesn't bother me.'

Involuntarily she meshed with those astonishingly blue eyes.

'It does have a certain novelty value,' he pointed out smoothly.

'Good,' she managed, and hurriedly smothered a yawn.

An odd slanting smile curved his expressive mouth. 'Start worrying if the novelty value starts to pall,' he advised.

It was three in the morning. Word games were beyond her. She propped her chin on her hand. 'Where do I sleep?'

'Go back upstairs. I'll stay down here for a while.'

At the door she hesitated. 'A while?'

He groaned impatiently. 'Look, I refuse to knock Hamish and Floss up in the middle of the night. That's a big bed up there. I shall lie down fully clothed on my half——'

'You can't!' Chrissy was livid at the very idea.

'I'm damned if I'm sleeping on the floor. Don't be such a prude, Chrissy. You won't know I'm there.'

Her lips tautly compressed, she stared back at his shuttered features. And then she sighed, all out of fight. It was a very big bed. He was clothed. She was practically asleep standing up. Furthermore, she'd be up long before he was in the morning...

The loud slam of a door woke her up the next day. As she sat up, shaking her heavy head to clear it, the bedroom door swung wide. It hadn't been properly closed. A girl clad in dirty jodhpurs and riding boots hurried across the room and lifted an executive case off the top of the chest of drawers. She didn't see Chrissy until she turned back towards the door. It would have been hard to estimate which of them was the most embarrassed.

'Sorry, I...I mean, I didn't know there was anyone...'
The girl stared at the heap of discarded male clothing
on the floor, averted her attention from it and Chrissy
both, and added, 'The guv'nor told me to fetch this.'

'Fine...OK,' Chrissy muttered awkwardly as the
brunette backed speedily out again.

Casting an aghast glance at the imprint of another
head on the pillow beside hers, Chrissy cursed herself
for not making use of her alarm clock the night before.
She didn't need to wonder what that girl had thought.
It had been written on her face. Looking at her watch,
she registered that it was after nine. Blaze would naturally have assumed that she was already up.

Springing out of bed, Chrissy tore off her nightshirt
and dressed at speed in black leggings and a black
sweater. 'Time to get up, Rosie!' she gasped.

She had assumed that her sister was still sleeping, but
the *chaise-longue* was empty. It was one shock too many.
Screaming, 'Rosie!' like a maniac, Chrissy's first stop
was the huge hole at the far end of the landing. She tore
about, throwing doors wide in search, before finally
flying breathless into the empty kitchen. And then she
saw them in the busy yard through the window. Blaze
was holding Rosie's hand while he stood talking to
Hamish.

'I'll take her now.' Her cheeks burning, Chrissy ad-
vanced on the two men.

'Good morning, Miss Hamilton,' Hamish said
woodenly.

Across the yard, the brunette and another stable girl
had their heads close together, two pairs of eyes watching
Chrissy's every step. The knowledge of what was
probably being said doubled her embarrassment. 'I'm
sorry I s-slept in,' she said.

'I owed you a lie-in and it was only half-five. Floss
gave us breakfast,' Blaze drawled as she lifted her sister.

'Did you dress her?' she asked as Hamish walked away.

'You must be joking. I grabbed a few likely-looking items and Floss came to the rescue. She loves kids; never had any of her own.' Blaze followed her back into the house. 'She offered to hang on to her while you do the shopping.'

'That's very kind of her but——'

'She reminded me that there was no car seat in the Land Rover——'

'But it's only two miles to the vill——'

'No.' The negative cut her off midflow. 'You don't take risks like that if you want to work for me. Is that clear?'

Chrissy bridled. Her protest had been powered by her reluctance to take any further advantage of this Floss, who was presumably Hamish's wife. This was her first day in the job and already she had fallen down on it. She should have been up early, seeing to Rosie and figuring out how to supply breakfast. 'Yes.'

'The garage at the crossroads has a car shop. They might have a car seat. If they don't, you'll have to go into Reading.' He withdrew his wallet and settled a handful of notes on the table.

Her teeth clenched. 'I'm going to *owe* you a month's wages by the time you pay me!'

'You're no use to me if you're not mobile.' He tossed her a set of car keys. 'And you can't go around penniless for the next month. You can pay me back in instalments once you get on your feet again.'

Studying the floor, she forced out one word. 'Thanks.'

'When you get back, find out where my furniture is. The number's underlined on the pad.'

It killed him to be thanked. As she tidied herself upstairs, Chrissy realised just how much she was in his debt. He was giving her a chance when most people wouldn't have bothered. He was making it possible for them to survive. Why? She couldn't help questioning his motives. He was nobody's idea of the good Samaritan. Did he feel sorry for them? Or did employing a Hamilton in a menial position amuse him? When her father found out, he would go mad.

'Anybody home?'

A plump woman with greying blonde hair stood in the hall. 'I'm Floss, Hamish's wife. I didn't half give him stick for not at least bringing you in for a cup of tea last night.'

And that was Floss, as warm and friendly as her husband had been cold. Within minutes, she was helping to bundle Rosie into her jacket as with Chrissy's agreement she planned to take her back to the greater comfort of the lodge.

'I feel terrible, landing you like this,' Chrissy confided.

'Don't be daft,' Floss said quietly. 'You concentrate on getting this place organised. Blaze…well, he's a good boss but he does expect results.'

Chrissy tautened, appreciating that she was being warned. 'I'm surprised he didn't offer you the job,' she remarked.

'He did but I wasn't having it.' Floss laughed. 'The hours he keeps, you'll be working all hours when he's here. Something part-time, though, I wouldn't have minded that,' she admitted. 'But not full-time.'

A brand-new Land Rover Discovery was parked in front of the Hall. It wasn't the vehicle Hamish had brought them here in the night before.

'Is this what I'm to use?' Chrissy breathed in dismay.

'Can't you manage it?' Floss looked anxious.

Ridding herself of the image of the small elderly run-about she had expected to drive, Chrissy climbed into the Land Rover. 'I'll get the hang of it,' she said with determination.

It was a beautiful car, larger and more powerful than anything she had ever driven before, and halfway to the garage she began to enjoy herself. The joy of renewed mobility was seductive. But the cost of the one car seat on offer in the shop brought her down to earth again with a bump. She would have expected a gilded throne for that amount. A week's wages, she thought, and she had so many other things to buy.

The village of Sotton was generally unchanged. The local pub had been tarted up and renamed, and the once tiny supermarket had moved site into larger premises. It was a relief to see no familiar faces inside it. She loaded a trolley with practically everything that took her eye, whizzed through the checkout, and was piling the last bag into the car when disaster struck.

'Chrissy...?' a female voice said faintly, incredulously.

She spun round, her hand on the tail-gate. Her sister, Elaine, was gaping at her from the lowered window of a white Porsche. Even as she spoke, she was climbing out. 'I can't believe it's you!' she exclaimed. 'What the heck are you doing up here?'

'The shopping.' Chrissy slammed down the tail-gate. 'How are you? Is Steve with you?' Bending, she peered into the Porsche in search of her brother-in-law.

Elaine made a little moue of distaste. 'No, of course he's not. The shopping?' she repeated irritably. 'For whom are you shopping?'

'I've got a job as a housekeeper locally.' Chrissy decided to give her the bad news all at once.

'Good God.' Elaine's perfect face was a mask of horrified disbelief. 'You can't be serious. Please tell me you're not serious,' she begged.

Chrissy was pale. 'Look, I've got to get back. I'd appreciate it if you didn't drop this on Dad unless you have to...'

'Oh, I'll leave that to you entirely,' Elaine said with ripe sarcasm. 'I was able to tell him that Belle was dead without a moment's hesitation, but this... this is like a dirty joke without the punchline! Are you out of your mind? Taking a job as a housekeeper?'

'Actually I'm more of a cook than a housekeeper.' Chrissy's stomach was heaving at Elaine's caustic, unfeeling reference to their mother's death. She could as

easily have been talking about a cousin three times re-
moved whom she had never met.

'Park over at the pub. I'll buy you a drink,' Elaine
instructed, tight-mouthed.

'I don't have the time——'

'Make the time. If you don't, I'll go straight back
home and tell Dad,' she threatened, her five-foot-ten-
inch model-slim figure taking on a positively aggressive
stance.

The threat worked. Chrissy knew that sooner or later
her father would find out where she was, but she was
keen to put off the evil hour as long as possible. Very
probably, Jim Hamilton would come roaring over to the
Hall to make a big scene and, when that did happen,
she wanted to be a lot more secure in her employment
than she currently felt.

She watched Elaine up at the bar, flicking her silver-
blonde hair back over her designer-clad shoulders, con-
fidently aware that the few male eyes in the place were
firmly pinned to her. She looked terrific, but then she
always had. Like Rory, she had inherited their mother's
looks. Some perverse trick of fate had endowed Chrissy
with her grandmother's colouring and five-foot-two-inch
stature. Nobody seeing them together, she conceded,
would ever take them for sisters.

It was a reaction she had often endured, from
childhood right up until she left home: the surprise as
she was unfavourably compared to her older sister. Even
her mother had not been untouched by that disappointment. 'It's such a pity you don't take after Elaine
and me,' she had once sighed.

Chrissy had been an accident, not a planned pregnancy. Elaine was ten years her senior, Rory twelve, and
the age-gap had meant that she'd been a solitary child,
most often made to feel a nuisance by her older siblings.
She had taken to comfort eating around puberty and the
surplus flesh had slowly piled on, ironically making her
feel more secure. It was almost as though she had wanted

to make herself as unattractive as possible, but in her teens, when her classmates were finding boyfriends, it had begun to hurt. She had started and stopped crash diets with monotonous regularity. It had taken Blaze to make her go green at the sight of chocolate.

Waiting for Elaine one day, he had strolled into the kitchen and found Chrissy tucking into a chocolate torte. 'You should put that down the waste disposal and padlock the fridge,' he had drawled, lounging up against the table, impossibly handsome, impossibly lean, as he'd surveyed her with almost morbid fascination. 'Or *are* you trying to eat yourself to death?'

'She's as fat as a pig, but Granny was as well.' Elaine had laughed from the doorway. 'I just cringe at the thought of looking like Chrissy.'

'Eating won't bring your mother back,' Blaze had murmured flatly, too perceptive for his own good even then.

Elaine slid on to the velour seat beside Chrissy, shooting her back to the present. 'Why are you doing this to us?' she demanded. 'Belle made us enough of a laughing-stock.'

'I needed work and this was the only work I was offered.' Chrissy lifted the uniced Coke which was all her sister had felt disposed to treat her to. 'Is Steve down with you?'

'I've left him ... Oh, he doesn't know it yet.' Elaine met her shocked gaze with faint amusement and tilted her chin. 'When the time's right, I'll tell him.'

'I'm sorry——'

'Don't be. I'm not. I let him think I was just coming down on an extended visit to Dad, but I have no plans to return to Edinburgh. Sooner or later, Steve will work it out for himself,' she said carelessly.

Chrissy had liked her brother-in-law. Three years ago, he had seemed to be a kind, thoughtful man, wholly suited to his career as a family GP and absolutely besotted with Elaine even when she was in her most dif-

ficult moods. 'What went wrong?' she pressed with
genuine concern.

Elaine shifted a shoulder. 'Nothing really. Money was
a problem, but until recently Dad always helped out...'

'And now he's stopped?'

'Well, he's been unbelievably stingy, although that has
nothing to do with why I left Steve,' Elaine asserted.
'No, I made that choice the instant I heard that Blaze
was moving back——'

'B-Blaze?' Chrissy echoed in stunned surprise, unprepared for his entry into the proceedings.

With a brilliant smile, Elaine leant back in her seat,
pleased to have drawn such a strong reaction. 'I intend
to get him back——'

'What?' Chrissy broke in again, her incredulity
unfeigned.

'Don't think I can't do it. I just messed up the last
time. I was too impatient. This time I'll be a lot more
careful, believe me,' she swore.

Chrissy took a deep breath. 'Elaine, it's over four years
since you went out with him, and even then it didn't last
long——'

'You don't know what split us up. I want him back.
I was crazy to marry Steve on the rebound. Blaze would
soon have forgotten that business with the old man,'
Elaine contended sharply, defensively. 'It wasn't our fault
and it wasn't even as if Blaze was particularly fond of
the old——'

Frowning, Chrissy interrupted, 'What old man?'

Elaine tensed, her eyes narrowing. 'How did we get
on to this subject? It's nothing to do with you.'

'I would like to know what you're talking about.'

'Ancient history that's none of your business.'
Hurriedly finishing her drink, Elaine stood up. 'You still
haven't told me who you're working for.'

'Nobody you know.' And she didn't know Blaze, never
had known Blaze, Chrissy found herself thinking with
surprising ferocity. Elaine talked now as though that brief

fling with him had been the love-affair of the century. Nobody but Elaine had thought that. And of course their father. Elaine was his favourite and he had been ambitious for her. It had never occurred to him that Elaine might ultimately meet with rejection. When Blaze had dropped her sister, Jim Hamilton had been shattered. He had taken it as a personal slight, a humiliating put-down.

'So he doesn't think you're good enough for him, does he?' Chrissy had heard him rage. 'If I ever get the chance, I'll show him, I'll bloody show him what a Hamilton's made of!'

'Don't be so childish,' Elaine snapped.

Chrissy had an alarming vision of being used as an excuse for Elaine to pursue Blaze. She cringed at the idea. Elaine was as relentless as a pitbull. She had caught Blaze the last time by popping up virtually everywhere he went. People had laughed at her but Elaine hadn't cared. She had wanted Blaze and she had got him even if she hadn't got him for as long as she had counted on. The end always justified the means in Elaine's book.

'If you don't know, you won't be tempted to tell Dad,' Chrissy said levelly.

'I don't really care. I was hardly planning to come visiting,' Elaine told her thinly. 'You can't be this poor, surely?'

'Offering me a loan?'

'Hardly.' Money might drain through Elaine's fingers like water, but she was not given to charitable impulses.

Chrissy sighed. 'I suppose I ought to tell you. I needed the job because I have a child to keep.'

Halfway back into the Porsche, Elaine froze and stared at her in horror. 'A child?'

'A child,' Chrissy confirmed.

'How could you be so stupid?' Elaine practically spat at her. 'You really do want to let us down a bucketful, don't you? As if Belle wasn't bad enough!'

Chrissy drove back to Westleigh with a lot on her mind. Elaine had presented her with a mystery. What business with the old man? What hadn't been whose fault? Elaine had spoken of fault in the plural. She had also said that Blaze wasn't that fond of the old man. That rather narrowed the field. Could Elaine have been referring to the late Lord Whitley, Blaze's grandfather?

But, strive as she might, Chrissy couldn't see any further connection. The old earl had died of a heart attack about two months after Blaze had ditched her sister. Chrissy had been finishing her last term at boarding-school during that period. Elaine had had her wedding the week after Lord Whitley had been buried, and it had been that same week, Chrissy reluctantly re-called, that she had stumbled quite accidentally on Blaze and learnt to her cost that people weren't always grateful for help and understanding.

Hamish barred her attempt to drive to the back of the Hall. 'Only horse-boxes are allowed in the yard,' he told her fiercely.

'I'm sorry.' For Floss's sake, she forced a placatory smile.

'The guv'nor's looking for you,' Hamish snorted.

She got halfway through the front door when a tall man with fair hair appeared out of a doorway and reached out to take her bags. 'Here, let me help you.'

Smiling at the pleasant stranger, she said, 'I'll go and grab another two.'

'I'm Pierce Balfour, one of your new neighbours.' Transferring the bags to one hand, he extended the other. 'And you can only be Chrissy——'

'Perhaps while you're trying to chat her up, Pierce, you might enquire what she was doing in the pub during working hours?'

Chrissy collided with icy sapphire-blue eyes and gulped. 'I was only in there ten minutes——'

'Hamish saw you.' Lounging in the doorway, Blaze dealt her a grim appraisal. 'You kick up your heels on your own time, not mine.'

'It won't happen again,' she muttered tightly.

'When are you on your own time?' Pierce inserted with interest. 'New faces are at a premium round here. I'd like to take you out to dinner.'

'She comes complete with passion-killing toddler,' Blaze drawled with sardonic bite. 'And right now she doesn't have any time of her own.'

Her cheeks burning, her temper on a short fuse, Chrissy reached for the bags Pierce had taken and marched them down to the kitchen. On her way back for the next two, she heard Pierce saying rather uncertainly that this wasn't the nineteenth century and had he been joking about the toddler? On her next passage past, she had to strain to catch Blaze enumerating the lethal dangers of endeavouring to have a casual affair with a single mother. Such women got too attached too quickly, clung like superglue and made you feel a heel by the end of it.

Fizzing with rage, Chrissy unpacked the groceries in record time. She couldn't remember when she had last had a date. Just as well. After that little lot, Pierce would take cover if she so much as looked in his direction! Whoever had said that women were the worst gossips had got it wrong.

She recognised Blaze's footsteps. She didn't turn round. 'Do you want lunch?' she asked icily.

'I said it for your own good. I was thinking of Rosie. He doesn't like kids.' His lazy drawl was quite unapologetic.

'Lunch?' she repeated rawly.

'You shouldn't hang around the pub either. It'll give the locals the wrong idea about you.'

That was it. Chrissy whirled round, hair flying, and fixed him with a shimmering look of loathing. 'I was not hanging around the pub!' she blistered back. 'And

I d-don't want or n-need your interference in my personal life!'

'Your personal life is an unholy mess,' he murmured drily. 'You need all the interference you can get.'

'Really?' She was shaking with anger, frustrated suddenly by her inability to tell the truth about Rosie's parentage. 'What you're saying is that my l-life is a mess because I have Rosie... Did your mother feel the same way about you?'

He didn't bat a single lush dark eyelash. 'My mother was two weeks off her wedding when she found my father in bed with his secretary. She might have cancelled the nuptials but she never got over him,' Blaze volunteered with astonishing cool. 'When I was five, she told me that Jaime was the only man she'd ever loved, but that didn't stop her from jumping into bed with every passing stranger in the hope of replacing him.'

Chrissy had paled, her anger mysteriously ebbing away. She was dismayed on his behalf, shocked that he could be so frank. She knew precious little about Lady Barbara Kenyon. She had died long before they'd moved to Berkshire, leaving Blaze to be brought up by his grandfather. But, come to think of it, she did vaguely remember someone once saying of Blaze that he was 'wild like his mother'.

'What age were you when she died?' she heard herself ask.

'Eleven.'

'What were you like?' Helplessly she studied him, searching that beautiful bone-structure for a shadow of the child he had been.

'Too pretty for my own good,' Blaze mocked. 'I was thrown out of every major and minor public school between here and Land's End. I had to be tougher than all the rest to survive.'

There was a curious stillness between them. She was thinking that there was nothing pretty about him now. Maturity had toughened those still startling good looks with a raw masculinity and blatant self-assurance that gleamed like polished steel. But still she was disturbed by that glimpse of just how alone he must have been as a child. She was beginning to understand where the cynicism came from.

'Hell, you're compassionate too,' Blaze drawled softly, reading her vividly expressive face with lazy amusement. 'You're like chocolate with a melting centre—all soft and warm. Be warned that most men with sob stories are trying to get laid.'

She was infuriated by the rush of heat she could feel surging up beneath her fine complexion. 'H-hardly in this instance,' she managed.

'If I didn't know better, I'd think you were a virgin,' Blaze mused, subjecting her to a mortifyingly intense appraisal. 'But then the only place you'd find a virgin of your age these days is in a convent ...'

'Tell me ... do you have to bring s-sex into every dialogue?' Bravely, she raised her chin on the dry challenge.

He burst out laughing. 'I could never understand why your family made such a thing of your stammer! I find it really appealing. As to why s-sex wandered into the dialogue, surely that's obvious? It was on my mind.'

Cursing her skin colouring, Chrissy found it necessary to turn away. Her stammer appealing? A most novel viewpoint from a male who was so famed for his penchant for incredibly beautiful and flawless women. He was teasing her, playing with her, like an embarrassing older brother, she told herself. He thought she was a prude about sex because she still blushed like an adolescent. It amused him. That was all.

It would probably amuse him even more if he realised that he had been spot-on as regarded her sexual status. Then she had not exactly been spoilt for choice or opportunity. Had she stayed on at college, she might have met someone, but Rosie had put paid to such freedom. In addition, both her mother's and Elaine's experiences would have put a guard on her own behaviour. It really wasn't a very good idea to leap into bed with someone you didn't know very well. Indeed, these days, it could well be a life-threatening experience.

'Floss is coming to your rescue,' Blaze murmured, his tone oddly harsh. 'Around me, Chrissy, strive to recall that I'm a bastard by birth *and* by nature.'

'I'm not in any danger of forgetting that,' she said breathlessly, but she was, because he was confusing her, blurring her image of him, once so starkly drawn. She really didn't know what he was likely to do or say next. He still wasn't keeping to the boundaries she had expected, and he had to be incredibly conceited to think that he had to keep on warning her off.

'I'll skip lunch. I'm off to Newmarket for a couple of days. The builders will be back on Monday. Keep an eye on them and . . . yes, the furniture is now due this afternoon. Decide where it's all going to go . . .'

As Floss came through the door with Rosie, Chrissy turned. 'You want me to decide?'

Blaze elevated a winged dark brow. 'I don't want to be hassled,' he told her. 'All I want you to do is turn this place into a comfortable home.'

'*All*?' she repeated. 'I'm not qualified to do that! You need an interior designer . . .'

'The door's already been shown to two of them.' Floss entered the conversation with humour.

'And you think that I could do better?' Chrissy demanded of Blaze.

'I don't see how you could do worse. You could pick out a kitchen,' he informed her with rampant impatience. 'Something suitable.'

'But I don't know what you think is suit——'

Hamish cut her off. 'Ready, guv'nor?'

Dazedly, Chrissy watched them head out. Her head was spinning.

'Show him a horse or a woman and he's in his element. Show him a house and he can't get out the door quick enough.' Floss laughed. 'He wants you to wave a magic wand for him.'

I'd sooner break it over his head, Chrissy reflected in exasperation. When it was obvious that he had strong likes and dislikes, he had no right to land her with such a task! She didn't want that responsibility. Mind you, if it hadn't been for that angle, she might have thought the prospect would be tremendous fun.

'I'm sorry about Hamish.'

Chrissy tensed as Floss gave her a rueful look. 'It's because of who your dad is. It's not personal, like, not really,' she insisted uncomfortably. 'But you see, Hamish and I worked for Lord Whitley all our married life. He was a decent old stick even if he was difficult. He didn't deserve to be taken advantage of like that——'

'Like what?' Chrissy prompted. She didn't know what the older woman was talking about but she desperately needed to find out.

Floss frowned. 'You don't know...you *really* don't know?'

'I haven't a clue what you're talking about,' Chrissy admitted. 'But please, I'd like to know.'

Floss sighed and looked uneasy. 'I wouldn't have mentioned it if I'd known. Hamish could tell you I was born with my foot in my mouth. Don't worry about him. He'll come round to you. He's just a stubborn old cuss——'

Chrissy wanted to scream her impatience. 'Floss, what has my dad to do with Lord Whitley?'

'It's not my place to tell you,' Floss said, her discomfiture unhidden as she moved towards the back door. 'And don't you be asking Blaze. There's no sense in stirring him up again, no sense at all. You don't need to worry about it anyway. Blaze wouldn't have given you the job if he'd held it against you.'

Floss was immovable. Clearly she believed that she had been dangerously indiscreet and nothing short of an earthquake was going to budge her from that position.

Chrissy, plundering her memory for even a shadow of vital information that she didn't have, watched Floss leave with an explosive sense of frustration.

Don't ask Blaze! Well, she hoped it wouldn't come to that but, one way or another, she had to get to the bottom of the mystery for her own peace of mind. What hadn't Blaze held against her? Something sufficiently serious and unpleasant enough to silence the effervescent and friendly Floss... undoubtedly the same something that her sister, Elaine, had been so determined not to discuss. And that in itself was worrying. As a rule, Elaine was refreshingly frank about her darkest doings.

CHAPTER FOUR

CHRISSY was dressing Rosie when Blaze strolled into the kitchen. Startled, she fumbled with the last button on her sister's sweater before she straightened, murderously conscious of the short, faded nightshirt she wore and the wildly curling tangle of hair she had not yet managed to comb. 'When did you get b-back?'

Rosie, whooping with noisy toddler pleasure, threw herself at Blaze. He scooped her up with a soft laugh of amusement. 'Late last night.'

Chrissy skimmed an uneasy hand over a slender hip. Brilliant blue eyes were trained on her and she flushed. 'I dress her down here because it's warmer...'

'Did I say there was a problem?' For a split-second, his jewelled gaze probed her with disturbing intensity.

She felt hot all over. 'I'll get dressed and make breakfast,' she mumbled, moving past him in a rush.

'No hurry. I'm curious...' At the top of the stairs, she halted and reluctantly turned as he drew level with her in one graceful step.

'About w-what?' Her fine brows had a pleat of anxiety now.

'About this.' He stilled in the open doorway of his bedroom. 'How did you do it?'

'Do what?' she prompted as she reached for Rosie, but Rosie wouldn't come.

Blaze planted a hand to her taut spine and propelled her deeper into the room. 'I was tempted to tip you out of bed in the early hours and ask you——'

'Ask me what?' Her small teeth worrying at her lower lip, she spread a troubled glance round the carefully furnished room in search of some glaring oversight that might have attracted his attention. She had spent all day

63

yesterday on this one room, picking out the pieces from the truly staggering amount of antique furniture and boxes that had been unloaded two days earlier. It had never occurred to her that he might own such a vast amount of furniture.

'Floss was never in my bedroom at the Manor in her life, so it wasn't her,' Blaze drawled. 'So how did you do it? I was staggered when I walked in here last night. This may be a different house, but this is an exact replica of the room I grew up in... Hell, you even have the same ornaments on the mantelpiece!'

Horror had frozen Chrissy to the spot. She was paralysed, her shocked gaze glued to the fine Dresden figurines he had indicated with an incredulous hand. A shudder ran through her. She couldn't believe what she had done without being aware of it, subconsciously using photographic recall to recreate the room in which they now stood. She couldn't believe that she could have been that stupid...

'You can't have seen my bedroom at the Manor...'

Chrissy had lost every scrap of natural colour and she was trembling, tiny little tremors of shock powering through every inch of her body as she struggled to hold back an agonising replay of the past and simultaneously conceal the truth from him. Every aspect of his bedroom at the Manor was indelibly stamped into her memory banks. Unable to look at him, she parted her dry lips. 'Oh, b-but I d-did!' she gasped in a fearful rush. 'One of th-those t-tours on an open day.'

'Our private rooms were never on view.'

'I s-saw it,' she insisted in desperation, wishing the ground would open up and swallow her.

'Are you feeling sick?' Blaze demanded abruptly. 'You look ghastly.'

She heard someone on the stairs and spun round to greet the interruption with gratitude. Hamish paused in the doorway. He slung her a scandalised look from fiercely narrowed eyes and his mouth closed tight as a coffin lid as he pointedly glanced away.

'Chrissy?' Blaze prompted.

Flushed to the roots of her hair by a tide of burning pink, Chrissy grabbed Rosie and ducked past Hamish. 'I'll g-get breakfast on!'

'Get dressed first,' Blaze advised carelessly. 'No need to give the builders a cheap thrill.'

She had to splash her face with cold water to cool down. Had she known he was back, she would never have come downstairs other than fully dressed! He had made it sound as though she was flaunting herself! But that mortifying reflection paled to nothing beside that glare of moral outrage on Hamish's horribly expressive face. He had surprised her in her nightie in Blaze's bedroom. Her goose was now cooked with Hamish for all time.

Blaze, evidently oblivious to the atmosphere, sat down at the kitchen table to eat what could only be described as a working breakfast with Hamish opposite.

'The Jockey Club...champion hurdler...novice chase...summer at grass...Sandown...' The unfamiliar terminology of the racing world drifted past her in snatched phrases as she quietly topped up the men's coffee and got on with the dishes. It was an effort to keep her hands steady. Deep down inside she was still breaking up. Blaze had put a crack in the dam wall she had built three years ago. Behind it she had carefully buried the debris of that long-ago night.

But it was coming back whether she wanted it to or not. It had been the night before Elaine's wedding. Chrissy had been driving back from checking the flowers in the church and she had taken a short-cut through the rarely used back entrance of Torbald Manor. It had shaved four miles off her journey.

Round the first corner on that private lane, she had had to jump on her brakes. A silver Porsche with its bonnet scrunched up against a huge oak tree had blocked

her passage. Naturally she had recognised the car and
naturally, like any good citizen, she had stopped at what
was clearly the scene of an accident. Her heart in her
mouth, she had peered into the dark interior, but the
car had been abandoned.

On her way back to her own car, she had heard the
sound of glass shattering somewhere near by. She should
have ignored it, minded her own business. Later she had
told herself that. Instead, in the best tradition of inter-
fering busybodies, she had walked off the lane into the
trees. It had been a clear, moonlit summer's evening,
warm enough for bare arms and a light dress. She had
found Blaze slumped beneath a tree, shivering as though
he were in a force-ten gale and freezing. There had been
a thin trail of blood on his temples and a blackening
bruise. A whisky bottle had lain broken several feet away
and even in the open air the smell of booze had been
powerful.

Although she would never have approached Blaze in
normal circumstances, the situation had urged her to take
charge. 'You've had an accident...you need a
doctor——'

'This is private property.' There had been a slight but
definite slur, marring those invariably clipped vowels.
'Go to hell!'

'I can't leave you here like th-this,' she objected
vehemently.

'Why not?' Angling his tousled dark head up with a
groan of discomfort, he focused on her with feverishly
glittering eyes.

'I just can't! You've had an accident——'

'So?' An insolent brow quirked with innate superiority.

'You should be in hospital, and you shouldn't have
been drinking in your condition.'

'Sorry, Nanny...will strive harder tomorrow.'

He looked so staggeringly vulnerable in spite of the
backchat. Unexpectedly, her eyes prickled with moisture
as she recalled that he had just buried his grandfather.

Clearly he was upset. Clearly, contrary to all the reports that he and the old man had rejoiced in mutual hatred, he was distressed by his grandfather's death. She crouched down beside him. 'I'm really sorry a-about your loss,' she said awkwardly.

'Loss? That's a lower-middle-class euphemism if ever I heard one! If I post the old boy as a missing person, do you think it would bring him back?'

'I didn't mean to be c-clumsy.'

'I'd like to say sorry,' he whispered as if she weren't there.

'I could go up to the Manor and call an ambulance.'

'Sorry for existing...always blamed me for that, never Barb. I was an immaculate conception, do you know that?'

'If you let me help you up, I could take you home,' she said in desperation.

'Women always want to take me home.' He was shivering more violently than ever. 'And I don't even know you.'

In the state he was in, he hadn't recognised her and, oddly enough, that knowledge made her bolder. Reaching down, she planted a determined hand on his arm. 'Come on,' she pressed bossily. 'I'll take you back up to the Manor.'

'Cold,' he admitted.

He staggered upright at her urging but half fell against her, pinning her between the tree and his own hard body. With difficulty she extricated herself and directed his faltering steps back to the lane. He got into her car with surprising docility and she drove on to the grass verge to get past the Porsche.

Torbald Manor was in complete darkness. She rang the antiquated front bell.

'Nobody in,' he mumbled. 'Sent everyone home.'

'Have you a key?'

She got him into the house through the rear courtyard. A maze of passages finally brought them into the vast front entrance hall. He collapsed at the foot of the stairs, seriously worrying her. Coaxing him upright again took time and she helped him upstairs, digging directions out of him to find his bedroom. There, she gratefully espied a phone and was in the very act of dialling the local doctor when Blaze abruptly realised who she was.

'Good God,' he slurred, reaching for her without warning. 'It's little Chrissy Hamilton...and to think that I had you down as shy!'

'I d-don't know what you're talking about.' Struggling to pull free of the frighteningly strong grip of those hard hands, she gasped, 'You're hurting me!'

'And that wasn't supposed to be part of the experience?' He laughed derisively, scanning her hotly flushed face with feverishly bright eyes. 'Chrissy Hamilton in my bedroom, desperate to play nurse... surprise...surprise,' he gibed thickly.

Almost hypnotised by his brilliant gaze and trembling, she mumbled, 'I don't understand——'

He yanked her closer, his wide mouth clenched in a savagely hard line. 'Save the game-playing for the teenage boys, sweetheart... You think I don't know what you want?' he murmured with an insidious drugging sweetness at odds with that blatant stare. 'You think that those huge green eyes don't talk enough for you? When you look at me like that, I know exactly what you want...'

Her brain was sluggish, her physical response to his proximity already sentencing her to baffled paralysis while she struggled to comprehend what was wrong with her. The heat of his hard body was warming hers, the all-male scent of him in her nostrils, a crazily intimate experience. She was holding her breath as though she was afraid to breathe, every muscle in her slender length unnaturally taut, a throbbing tension entirely new to her making a nonsense of her ability to think.

And then he kissed her.

It sounded like a silly line in a song, she told herself, sinking back to the present with a deep shudder of recollection. And in the same moment she had been engulfed by raw sensation, so powerful and so overwhelming that she had lost control, surrendering herself utterly and completely to the rough, invasive heat of his hard mouth on hers. Seconds...that was all it had taken, seconds in which to learn that her body had feelings and desires quite divorced from the power of her intelligence. Never until that moment had she understood how devastating sexual desire could be, and that she should have had that humiliating discovery forced on her by Blaze Kenyon would have been punishment enough.

For he hadn't even *wanted* her! He had believed that she wanted him. He had been cruelly, coldly scoring a point. His look of revulsion as he'd thrust her back from him would live with her forever. He hadn't had to say that she was fat and utterly without the smallest attraction; that look had said it for him. Stumbling, she had fallen back against the bed and he had had her cornered. Then the verbal beating had begun and, throughout, stricken by horrified paralysis, she had cowered there, looking everywhere but at him, and somehow during those minutes every aspect of that bedroom had become brutally imprinted in her memory.

She had tried so hard not to listen but Blaze had been remorseless. He had told her that he wouldn't touch her with a barge-pole, that she was a very silly little girl, who had just made a gigantic fool of herself, and that if he had been in any fit state to drive he would have dragged her home and informed her father what she had been up to. Her father would have slaughtered her on the doorstep. In terror, she had shivered and shaken, making no attempt to defend herself, because her physical response to him had demolished her only defence in advance.

'Get the hell out of here,' he had finally slurred, staggering back as if he was finding it difficult to stay upright. And she had fled, sobbing and sick to the stomach with the taste of raw humiliation he had dealt out without quarter.

'Chrissy...are you OK?' Dragged from that nightmare of recollection, Chrissy flinched back in horror when her distant eyes focused abruptly on Blaze. 'What the hell is the matter with you this morning?' he demanded. 'I said I want lunch early.'

'F-fine,' she stammered.

His ebony brows drawn together in a questioning frown, he grabbed up his jacket and strode out, Rosie tagging at his heels.

Chrissy unfroze and raced out after them. 'Rosie!'

Blaze swung round. 'She can tag along for an hour, get some fresh air. I'll send her back pronto if she gets under my feet,' he asserted.

'The yard's no place for a child,' Hamish intervened, grim-mouthed.

'But this child lives here.' Blaze enveloped the five starfish fingers straining up to his hand with a cool air of finality. 'She might as well start learning what she does and doesn't do out here now.'

Chrissy gritted her teeth. Maybe Rosie's slavish adoration flattered him, but sooner or later her demands would irritate rather than amuse, and then Chrissy would be forced to play the bad guy, struggling to keep one very persistent toddler out of his hair. Didn't he realise what he was doing? Why was he encouraging Rosie? When Blaze got bored, her sister would be hurt.

She was baking when Hamish walked in, his weather-beaten face set in a pugnacious scowl. 'You think you're so clever,' he condemned fiercely, taking up a militant stance on the other side of the table. 'You've even fooled Floss. She always likes to think the best of people. She doesn't want to see what's going on under her nose——'

Her cheeks warming, Chrissy straightened. 'You mis-understood what you saw this morning, Hamish——'

'I'll give you a free word of advice,' Hamish cut in harshly. 'Get back to wherever you came from and stay there! You're not welcome here.'

The force of his loathing hit Chrissy hard. She was in shock. She had known that Hamish neither liked nor approved of them, but, naïvely, she had not been pre-pared for so open an attack. Pale and tense, she began, 'I th-think——'

'Yes, you sit down and you think hard. There'll be no rich pickings here for either you or your sister!' Hamish told her roughly. 'You had your lot when the old man died and there'll be no more. Don't you listen to Floss talking about forgiving and forgetting. Blaze hasn't forgotten. When your sister came dancing up to him at Newmarket, he played her like a fish on a line, just like he's playing you!'

'My sister?' Chrissy's head was spinning. 'Elaine was at N-Newmarket?'

'Aye, serving herself up on a plate,' Hamish imparted crudely.

Chrissy was shattered by the revelation that Elaine had already contrived to meet up with Blaze again. He hadn't mentioned the fact either. A deep flush banished her pallor, for she was mortified by the older man's de-rision. But that sensation was short-lived as she regis-tered that Hamish evidently cherished none of his wife's inhibitions about referring to whatever had happened three years ago.

'Rich pickings?' she repeated with as much dignity as she could muster. 'What on earth are you talking about?'

'Three years ago, your sister waited until Blaze was abroad and then paid a call on Lord Whitley with your father. All very friendly, it was, I'm sure,' Hamish sneered. 'It was easy to sucker in an old man in his eighties——'

'"Sucker in"?' she repeated unsteadily.

'You know exactly what they did!' he condemned bitterly.

'I genuinely d-don't!' Chrissy insisted hotly.

'Blaze had dumped her and she wanted her own back, was that it?' Hamish demanded fiercely. 'Everybody knew Lord Whitley liked a game of cards. The old boy was a gambler but he didn't have the money to back up some high-rolling poker game! Your father took him for thousands——'

Chrissy swallowed with difficulty. 'I don't believe you.'

'Between them, your father and your sister killed him,' Hamish condemned bitterly. 'Lord Whitley was a gentleman. He saw those losses as a debt of honour but he couldn't settle up. He didn't have the money and your father dunned him like a debt collector!'

'I d-don't believe you...I d-don't believe you,' Chrissy mumbled in shaken repetition.

'The shame and the worry of it all brought on that heart attack. He was a very healthy old man until that card game,' Hamish asserted wrathfully. 'He was too proud to ask Blaze for help, and ever since Blaze has blamed himself for bringing your sister into the old man's radius. That's how they talked their way through the door—using Blaze as a reference. Lord Whitley thought he was just playing a little poker with friends. He was eighty-five years old. It was a filthy, dirty scam! They couldn't touch Blaze, so they chose an easier prey——'

'No!' Chrissy raised unsteady hands to cover her damp, hot face. She felt physically sick. She wanted to say that she didn't believe it could have happened that way, but she couldn't forget how enraged her father had been when Blaze dropped Elaine. And when Jim Hamilton wanted to hurt anyone, he hit their bank balance. But to approach an old man with a known weakness for gambling with the deliberate intent of fleecing him ... and then to plague him to pay up money that he didn't have? Would even her father stoop that low? She didn't want to remember her father's bone-deep resentment of the upper classes. He had been born with it, and his loathing had intensified when many of those same people had repeatedly refused invitations to his home. Never had it occurred to him that it was his personality, not his background, which was his biggest handicap.

That loathing had gone underground when Blaze had started seeing Elaine. Jim Hamilton would have forgiven much had Blaze proved properly appreciative of his daughter's charms and married her. Indeed her father would have exulted in Elaine's becoming Mrs Blaze Kenyon. There would have been no more cracks about the upper classes then. But Elaine had been shot down in flames like so many ambitious girls before her.

White and trembling, Chrissy collided with Hamish's grim, unforgiving stare, wanting so badly to be able to defend her family but horribly aware that her father would have been perfectly capable of plotting such a revenge, and Elaine equally capable in her bitterness of colluding with him.

'If it wasn't for that wee lassie of yours, I wouldn't be warning you off,' Hamish admitted harshly. 'Blaze is a total bastard when he's crossed and he has a long memory. He'll break you and your precious sister before he's finished. If you can't see what's coming, you're a fool, and only a fool would ever have come up here!'

He left her standing there in a state of shock. Her mind could not yet embrace the full enormity of what her father and her sister stood accused of. Had they known that Lord Whitley wasn't a rich man? Chrissy hadn't known. She had simply looked at Torbald Manor and assumed that the Kenyons were wealthy, but, with the hindsight of maturity, she could appreciate that an ancestral home and a title did not necessarily mean a very large bank balance. The Kenyons might well have been struggling like so many other landed families simply to hold on to what they had and survive. And yet Blaze appeared to be anything but cash-poor now.

Then what relevance did that have to the past? It in no way condoned what her father and sister had done. Suddenly, Chrissy couldn't stand the suspense any longer. Washing the flour off her hands, she sped off to find Blaze.

She had to trek up to the jumps where the grooms were working the horses. It was a cold, crisp day with more than a hint of frost. The breeze clawed her hair into wild tangles. By the time she drew level with Blaze, she was shivering and wishing she had stopped to collect her coat on the way out.

'Kissy!' Rosie announced, yanking at the hem of his waxed jacket to attract his attention.

His dark head turned, impatience stamped on his striking features. 'What do you want?' he demanded bluntly. 'I'm busy.'

Briefly she studied her mud-caked shoes and then she threw her head back. If she didn't tackle him now, she might not get a chance later. The builders would be all over the house. 'I want to know——'

'Yes?' he prompted shortly.

'I...I want to know if it's t-true that my father took your grandfather f-for a lot of money in a poker game...and then pestered him for payment,' she shot at him in a stammering rush.

The brilliant sapphire eyes narrowed. Disorientatingly, there was no change of expression, nothing whatsoever to tell her whether or not she had taken him by surprise. 'You didn't know... Who told you?' he probed almost lazily.

'I d-don't think that's relevant...'

'Hamish,' he mused.

Her small hands clenched into fists. 'Is it true?'

'Forty thousand quids' worth of true,' Blaze told her, utilising the same disturbingly unemotional intonation.

'F-forty thousand pounds?' she gasped incredulously, unable to credit his apparent calm. 'There must have been some sort of misunderstanding——'

'No.' With that one silky word, he cut her off mid-sentence.

She collided with drowningly blue eyes and her throat closed over, making it hard for her to swallow. His expression hadn't changed but the temperature had dropped below freezing. It was like coming up smash-bang against a wall of ice. She found that she couldn't take her eyes off him. It was terrifying, chilling and yet oddly compulsive. Behind the ice burned a savagely implacable force of will intriguingly at war with the cool, dispassionate front he wore for the world.

It had been a mistake to tackle him without forethought. She had acted on impulse, something she did all too often, she conceded with exasperation. But she was still attempting to come to grips with what Hamish had told her.

'Satisfied?' he pressed impatiently, patently unconcerned by her visible distress.

'But you gave me a job,' she whispered in helpless bewilderment.

A broad shoulder lifted in an infinitesimal shrug. He quirked an ebony brow. 'So?'

Her cheeks reddened fiercely. He was well aware that she had had nothing to do with what had happened, yet did he really cherish no animosity towards her for the blood that ran in her veins? She wanted to smash the ice holding her at bay. She wanted to know how he really felt, and the snarling force of her own sudden frustration astonished her. She wanted the truth, not a macho pretence of indifference.

'It was a long time ago,' he murmured with silky emphasis.

'Don't do that!' she burst out, emerald-green eyes welded to him in raw frustration. 'Don't lie to me!'

A tiny muscle clenched taut at the corner of his wide, sensual mouth. Her percipience had surprised him. 'Why should I lie?' he demanded softly.

'I...I don't know.' Abruptly she raised unsteady hands and pushed her wildly blowing hair back from her wind-stung cheekbones, her beautiful eyes fixed pleadingly on his savagely handsome features. 'You s-stay away from my sister!' she told him with sudden ferocity.

His smile was one hundred per cent predator and it raised her hackles. That brilliant, edged smile told her all she didn't want to know. Modesty was not one of his virtues. He was fully aware of the effect he had on her sex. '*She's* very much in need of your advice.'

'But you must hate her!' Chrissy protested in disbelief.

'Is she worth that much emotion?'

Chrissy went white. A shiver of instinctive apprehension tautened her muscles. 'If you encourage her...'

'But I don't need to encourage her,' Blaze said softly.

'You'll wreck her marriage!' Chrissy condemned.

'This is turning into a very boring conversation.' Jewelled sapphire eyes rested on her with diamond-cutting chill. 'Stay out of what you don't understand.'

Chrissy was shaking all over. 'I understand you p-perfectly!'

'Where have you been all my life?' he drawled silkily. 'What ghastly trick of fate has placed you beneath my roof? The desire to be understood by a woman has never been one of my priorities.'

'You conceited t-toad!' Without any warning whatsoever, she found her emotions exploding out of her control. 'What w-would any intelligent woman want with you?'

'Bad girl, bad Kissy!' Rosie put in anxiously, abruptly recalling Chrissy to the fact of her presence and the knowledge that she was shouting. Stricken with guilt, she glanced down at Rosie's distressed little face.

'Relax, sweetheart,' Blaze soothed silkily, stroking a calming hand across her small head.

The blind adoration in Rosie's trusting gaze further outraged Chrissy. 'Don't touch her!' she spat.

'Mummy and I haven't kissed and made up yet,' Blaze murmured quietly, only the gleaming anger burnishing his eyes betraying his true mood.

'It'll be a cold d-day in hell——' Chrissy began hotly, but a split-second later the power of speech was torn from her. A hand like a steel clamp curved round her narrow shoulder, forcing her forward. His mouth came down on hers with similar force. It was violent. It should have been utterly repellent. But it wasn't. She flamed alive in an extraordinary surge of passion.

His tongue plundered the moist, sensitive interior of her mouth until every inch of her body was plastered to the hard, unyielding outlines of his. It was a flagrantly, ferociously sexual assault and it unleashed a tidal wave of response. She couldn't get close enough to him . . . he couldn't get close enough to her. He had her welded so tightly to him that she could barely breathe. Her hands sank into the thick luxuriance of his hair in an ecstasy of pleasure, tiny sounds ripping from her throat as long fingers knotted with painful thoroughness into the curling torrent of mahogany tumbling down her back. It was like being devoured . . . but it was a mutual feast.

Her every skin cell leapt with sensation. Her heartbeat thundered through her entire body. The blood in her veins raced and boiled. She wanted . . . dear lord, she craved . . . she needed . . . she had to have . . . *this*, this fierce, glorious intensity of feeling!

Abruptly, Blaze tore his mouth from hers. Two hard hands bit into her shoulders as he wrenched her back from him but retained his hold on her. A dark flush lay along the line of his carved cheekbones, his breath coming in tortured bursts as the stark brilliance of his astonishingly bright eyes focused on her hectically flushed face, arrowing down into glazed green, and later, much later, she would recall that for a tenth of a second he looked absolutely shattered.

And then dense black lashes veiled those unusually expressive eyes. 'I'll dump Rosie with Floss,' he murmured thickly. 'You chuck the builders out... Bloody hell, I'll pay them to get out and stay out for the rest of the day! Warm up the bed for me... I'll be as quick as I can.'

Her recovery time had been slower than his. Indeed, she had been so overwhelmed by the desire he had ignited inside her that she had been standing there with the docility of an accident victim. But the brutal candour he employed to state his intentions—indeed, his *expectations* not only shook her rigid, it shook her right back to normality.

'You... y-you... animal!' she gasped, pulling frantically free of his controlling hold. 'I can't believe you said that to me! How d-dare you? How dare you even think that I... that I would allow... that I would do something so utterly d-disgusting?'

He looked as if he wanted to kill her. He looked as he had no right to look. He looked outraged but, most insultingly of all, he looked as if he just couldn't believe that he was actually being turned down. One heated embrace and he expected her to spread herself on his bed without any further ado! She was the one, surely, with the right to look incredulous? If it hadn't been for Rosie, she would have punched him in the face!

Staggeringly out of her depth, assailed by a hideous surge of unpleasant emotions and an outsize awareness that that abandoned clinch had had a large and interested audience, Chrissy fumbled for and found her little sister's hand. When he touched her, the rest of the world just didn't exist. When he touched her, her self-control, her self-knowledge splintered. When he touched her, there was nothing and nobody but him and the most terrifying, devastating desire for him to continue. And right now she felt savaged, brutalised, and shamed by the awareness that she could not control her own sexuality.

There was nothing more to say. She was cringingly aware of that fact. Indeed, she couldn't make her escape quickly enough. How the heck could she continue to work for Blaze after this? The way she had responded to him... was it really any wonder that he had expected her to go to bed with him? She prided herself on her honesty. She had not given him any reason to believe that she was not willing to finish what he had begun. But he had shocked her, forced her to face the depth of her own ignorance.

Blaze lived on the fast track of a different world, unfettered by the inhibitions that haltered her. He had wanted to have sex with her. That was all. He hadn't wanted anything else. Just an available body to slake a hot-blooded surge of male hormones. She drove that harsh truth home to herself hard. And doubtless he would not understand how unbearably offensive that truth was to her. She had no ambition to be used for an afternoon of light entertainment and then discarded like yesterday's newspaper.

Dear heaven, how could she have allowed him to do that to her again? She blinked back hot tears of self-loathing. It seemed that she was more like her mother and Elaine than she had ever dreamt—lacking all control and pride, losing all judgement in the sheer heat of sexual desire. She had behaved like a tramp, she told herself fiercely, and it was hardly surprising that he had come to the same conclusion.

Hours later, when she was frantically trying to prevent the casserole she had prepared from drying up, Floss poked her head round the door and stared at the sight of the carefully laid table. 'Haven't you had lunch yet?'

'I'm waiting for B-Blaze.'

'Didn't he tell you?' Floss frowned in surprise. 'He's off to London.'

CHAPTER FIVE

CHRISSY was ready to tear out her hair and scream. During the night a pipe had burst, flooding the kitchen. The builders had dealt efficiently with the problem, but they had had to rip up the ancient quarry tiles to complete the task. They had put the tiles down loose as a temporary surface and they were absolutely filthy. The sodden contents of the lower cupboards were spread out everywhere. And the newly installed central heating was airlocked and inactive.

Her head was splitting from the noise of the sanding machines being used on two of the reception-rooms. She was wet and exceedingly dirty and, to crown it all, Rosie was down on all fours on that filthy floor pretending to be a horse.

'Get off that f-floor!' she launched at her little sister.

'Moo...moo.' Rosie pawed stubbornly at the tiles. 'Wanna carrot.'

'You are not a horse!' Chrissy practically screeched. She had never been so tired in her life. She had worked non-stop for a week and nowhere could she see results. Blaze hadn't been in touch and, when she had finally steeled herself to phone his London apartment, some manic bimbo had screamed abuse down the line at her as soon as she'd given her name, telling her to leave Blaze alone.

Suddenly Rosie gave a shout of ecstasy and galloped across the floor still on her knees. In mute dismay, Chrissy focused on the tall, dark figure lounging in the doorway. He looked so clean. There he was, framed like some impossibly perfect being in a glossy magazine, polished leather boots leading up to skin-tight cream riding breeches, an Aran sweater and an Australian stockman's full-length green coat, liberally spattered with crystalline raindrops. Extravagantly, sickeningly gorgeous, she acknowledged with gritted teeth and raw resentment.

'Wosie wanna carrot. Moo!' Rosie grinned up at him with eyes the size of saucers.

'Cows eat grass...'

'Horses eat carrot.' Rosie pouted.

He was deliberately ignoring her, Chrissy decided.

'I've actually been back a couple of hours,' he volunteered in a careless aside. 'I got changed and went out to check the yard. No problems there. Not quite so organised indoors from what I can see. Still, we all have our off days. Is lunch on the go?'

'L-lunch?' she practically whispered. He hadn't even bothered to tell her that he was back. He simply strolled in and criticised her when she had been working eighteen-hour days! Floss had suggested that she make dinner every evening just in case he came home. So far, she had cooked and dumped the greater part of five stylish dinners, calculated to impress the most demanding *bon viveur*. And now he rolled up without warning when the kitchen was in a state of the most unspeakable squalor and expected to be fed.

Right now, he was actually coaching Rosie on the vocal difference between a cow and a horse. She couldn't believe it. For a week she had tossed and turned in her bed and barely slept as she'd agonised over how he would behave and how she should behave when he finally reappeared. His air of careless insouciance made it patently clear that their clash a week ago had gone off him like water off a duck's back.

'There is no l-lunch,' she admitted shakily, closing her hands tightly together.

'Why not?' Sapphire-blue eyes awash with apparent incredulity flicked in her direction.

'Maybe Hamish would give *you* a bucket!' Chrissy suddenly snapped in a shatteringly loud rush, powered by an uncontrollable surge of anger.

'Excuse me for a moment.' Blaze hauled Rosie up into his arms, strode out to the yard with her and dumped her into Hamish's astonished grasp—Hamish who had clearly been hovering outside in the hope of hearing her get the sack.

'Why did you do th-that?' Chrissy almost shrieked.

'You're shouting. I don't want her upset. A bucket, you were saying,' he murmured, silkily sardonic.

'There's no water! And Hamish w-wouldn't let me have water from the yard because he says I spook the horses! And the electricity will be off again in ten minutes! Stuff your bloody lunch, you chauvinist dinosaur...who do you think I am? S-Superwoman?' she raged.

He spread a derisive glance round the chaos. 'Super-woman?' he said softly. 'Evidently not.'

And that was when she lost her head. She had been struggling to cope single-handedly with a squad of workmen ripping up floors and gouging holes in walls in umpteen different locations. They walked plaster all over the place. They didn't bother to cover the fur-niture. Dust lay an inch thick everywhere and he didn't even possess a vacuum cleaner!

She had the feeling that for all of his adult life women had been falling over themselves to do things for him. Not just in bed but out of it as well. He probably hadn't had to ask or demand. Boring, time-consuming things had been taken care of well out of his sight and hearing.

'While you were partying with your k-killer bimbo down in London, I have been working my ass off!' Her eyes were flaming emeralds in her hectically flushed face. 'You didn't keep in touch! You didn't leave me any money! You don't h-have a vacuum cleaner! You don't even h-have a washing machine! Two ceilings have come down since you l-left and today the kitchen flooded—— '

'God, this is my worst nightmare come true,' Blaze whispered. 'This feels like being married——'

'You sh-should be so lucky! You're the most self-centred, egotistical, impractical, s-s-s-sel—sel——'

'Selfish?' he threw in helpfully, one-hundred-megawatt attention fully attuned to her now.

'A-and,' she sobbed, tears taking over, 'I'm dirty and I've g-got no clean clothes!'

Silence fell, broken solely by the embarrassing sobs that had overcome her. Collapsing down on a chair, she buried her contorted face in her hands and fought unsuccessfully to stop crying.

'I can see that the mention of lunch was unfortunate,' Blaze conceded thoughtfully.

He scooped her out of the chair without warning. She didn't even fight. He was going to throw them out. He wasn't used to hearing home truths. He had probably never been so grossly insulted in his spoilt-rotten, selfish, hedonistic life.

But he didn't dump her on the doorstep. He stuffed her into the front of the Ferrari. 'W-where . . . ?' she managed on the back of another sob.

'I'm taking you down to the pub. I'll take a room and you can have a bath.'

He was utterly crazy. He couldn't be serious. But he was.

He raked to a halt at the rear of the Pheasant, angled an assessing glance over her tear-swollen profile, and sighed. 'When you cry, you really cry, don't you? You look like a battered pixie. We'll use the tradesman's entrance. Percy won't mind.'

He had to drag her from the car. She felt really stupid, mortified by her breakdown. He draped his coat round her quivering shoulders and the hem trailed on the tarmac.

'You'll feel a whole lot more human once you get a couple of stiff drinks inside you;' Blaze asserted.

'I d-don't drink...'

'Trust me, it'll transform your view of the world.' He left her huddled by the coats in the tiny back hall and disappeared. Two minutes later, he returned, swinging a key, and urged her upstairs.

'This is a-absolutely mad!' She hovered in the centre of the cosily furnished bedroom in a state of extreme discomfiture.

'You take life too seriously. I'll run your bath.' He strode into the adjoining *en suite*.

Tiny little shudders were still rattling through her. She wondered why she was letting him take control. 'Why are you doing this?'

'It'll make *me* feel better.'

An unsteady laugh escaped her. At least he was honest. 'There's too much work for me to do in that house,' she admitted shakily. 'It's too big. I c-can't keep up with the workmen...'

'No problem. I'll bring in a cleaning agency. All I ever expected you to do was cook and oversee the builders——'

'And arrange your furniture and decide where your sockets and radiators go, and your clothes, and choose your kitchen and your tiles and your wallpaper and...'

Lean hands reached down and slowly undraped the coat. As it fell in a pool round her paralysed feet, her voice ran out. Dazedly, drained by sheer exhaustion, she just stood there. Long brown fingers reached for the buttons on her shirt and abruptly she jerked away. 'I can manage...'

She was peeling off her clothes in the bathroom when Blaze opened the door six inches and set a balloon glass of brandy down on the floor. She surveyed it uncertainly, wondering whether it would settle the nausea in her stomach. Stepping into the bath, she downed it in one, choking as the unfamiliar alcohol burned her unprepared throat.

The hot water was bliss. The bubbles made her giggle. She felt like a five-year-old being coaxed out of the sulks. Yes, she reflected ruefully, he was truly in his element with a woman, and right now he was probably down in the restaurant perusing the menu for his lunch.

The door opened again just a little, not enough to panic her but enough to make her tense in dismay.

'Do you want another drink?'

'You c-can't come in and I'm too lazy to come out.'

'You really are the most amazing prude.' He rolled the bottle across the floor.

Chrissy giggled and reached for it with a 'what the hell?' feeling of decadence. Pouring herself another generous measure, she sank back into the scented water, literally feeling all the stress draining away.

'Who is the killer bimbo?'

She told him about the unproductive phone call. 'She was a m-maniac.'

Absolute silence.

'Are they all that intellectually challenged?' she couldn't resist asking.

'I don't sit them down to a Mensa test before I bed them,' he conceded reflectively.

'You sound very close,' she accused with sudden tension.

'I'm lying on the bed. Can't see a thing.' A pause. 'I only ever have one woman at a time. I don't sleep around.'

'You could lie your way round a lynch mob,' she murmured blithely, unconvinced. 'I feel so sorry for you——'

'And I just know you're about to tell me why.'

'Emotionally you're stunted——'

'Physically you're repressed.'

The brandy she was aiming at her lips missed and trickled down her throat into the water instead. She stopped breathing and then took another deep gulp of brandy.

'There's just something about you. I don't know what it is,' Blaze drawled with a silken relaxation that was positively predatory. 'But whatever it is...it's staggeringly sexual and it is creating problems. I want to make love to you. It would get it out of the way. Curiosity killed, we could then forget it ever happened.'

Silence stretched. Finally, he breathed, 'No comment?'

'To think I thought you'd be the last word in seduction!' Chrissy sighed in a tone of rampant disillusionment.

'I am trying very hard to be totally frank and not take advantage of your inexperience.'

Draining her glass, she slid clumsily upright, water sloshing everywhere. Her head was swimming. 'I c-can't even be offended. You're certifiable. You're a big disappointment too.' She lurched at the large bath-towel and caught it more by accident than design. 'You deserve the killer bimbo. I want wild passion. I want a lover who can't keep his hands off me. I want a guy who looks at me as if I'm Demi Moore, is hopelessly in love with my mind and still faithful after our ruby wedding anniversary...'

Hideously dizzy, she collided with incredibly blue eyes and swayed. 'H-he's out there somewhere...he just hasn't found me yet,' she asserted, slurring her words as she tripped over the trailing towel and fell flat at his feet with a resounding crash. 'If I thought you were all there was, I think I'd kill myself,' she concluded as she endeavoured to pick herself up.

'You are absolutely plastered,' he groaned, bending down to pick her up since she wasn't making much headway on her own. He looked down at her with an oddly arrested expression.

'P-paralytic!' She giggled and passed out.

*   *   *

'You should have told me that you hadn't eaten and that you had never had alcohol before.'

Wincing from her sore head, she muttered, 'Stop g-going on about it.'

Mercifully, it was dark as they left the Pheasant. He had let her sleep and then he had shaken her awake, presented her with her clothes, which he had had dry-cleaned, and a tray of food that had settled uneasily in her too empty stomach. Half an hour later, he had returned and hustled her out of the Pheasant at speed.

He drew up in front of the Hall and swung round to look at her. His expressive mouth suddenly slanted with raw amusement. 'Drunk... you're hilarious.'

Tense and miserable, she whispered, 'I made an idiot of myself.'

He expelled his breath. 'I rather think you made an idiot of me. But why no alcohol ever before?'

'My mother,' she responded tautly.

'But she loved a——'

'Yes, loved it a little too much when the going got rough.' She climbed out of the car.

Floss was comfortably ensconced by the fire in the small sitting-room. Rosie was watching a cartoon on the television. On the brink of offering a stammering apology, Chrissy was forestalled by Blaze.

'Just as you said, I've been working her to death.'

Floss nodded approval of the admission. 'And she hasn't been letting me help out with Rosie either,' she added, and Chrissy flushed, conscious that she had refused the older woman's assistance, fearful that Hamish might accuse her of taking advantage of his wife's good nature. 'I love looking after her,' Floss concluded wistfully.

When Floss had gone home, Chrissy went out to the kitchen. It was a disaster area, there was no escaping that fact, and with a sigh she rolled up her sleeves.

'Forget it; put your feet up,' Blaze drawled from the doorway. 'The cleaning agency are sending in a squad in the morning and they can come in every couple of days for as long as we have to live in this chaos.'

Chrissy spun round. 'But that will cost you a fortune!' she said guiltily.

'I can afford it,' he dismissed. 'You'll be free to focus your energies on more important things. You know, I never expected you to get down on your knees to scrub floors. To be truthful, I've never had to think of practicalities like that.'

He was gone again, but she still stared at the space he had occupied. Every time she thought she understood him, he side-stepped her and astonished her again. He could be so considerate, so gentle with Rosie, and yet she sensed that neither of those virtues coloured his relationships with women. At the Pheasant he had been brutally honest about his desire to make love to her. And even more brutally honest in the acknowledgement that it would lead nowhere.

Few men would have dared such candour. But Blaze had. Yet she could hardly believe that Blaze, who was famous for being able to get any woman he wanted with the barest minimum of effort, *could* actually desire her... Chrissy Hamilton, who had certainly never had any cause to think of herself as a *femme fatale*. He behaved as though she was incredibly desirable. Her brow furrowed, confusion making her head ache. At the back of her mind, she was trying not to recall Hamish's assurance that Blaze wanted revenge on the Hamilton family. Blaze had been extraordinarily kind to her and Rosie, flinging them a lifeline when they were absolutely desperate.

She was saying goodnight to Rosie when she heard the thumping on the front door. Taking the stairs two at a time, she answered it. A powerful hand slammed the door hard back against the wall, forestalling any attempt she might have made to deny entry.

'D-Dad!' she gasped in unconcealed horror, backing away fast.

Jim Hamilton lunged forward like a heavyweight boxer going in for the kill, his broad face crimson with menacing fury. 'So it's true!' he bit out, his big hands clenching into fists of rage. 'He has got you up here!'

'B-Blaze gave me a job——'

'A job? Is that what you call it? He gave you something else too, from what I've been hearing! You've got a kiddy the living spit of the bastard!'

Chrissy was as white as the newly plastered wall behind her, her stricken gaze pinned to him in consternation. 'Rosie isn't h-his!' she protested. 'I just work for him——'

'Work for him?' Jim Hamilton vented a harsh crack of incredulous laughter. 'On your back? Is that how you work for him? When you were laid up in the Pheasant with him all afternoon, were you working for him then? The whole bloody village is talking about it! Couldn't wait for the builders to get out, they're saying! Living up here in sin with a child into the bargain, calling yourself his damn housekeeper! You stupid little cow; didn't I teach you any better? I'll teach you better when I get you home, girl... by God, I will!' he threatened.

'I'm not g-going anywhere with you.' Appalled by the scene developing, Chrissy was equally appalled by the news that people were talking about her, making nonsensical assumptions about Rosie's parentage and even more embarrassing assumptions about the precise nature of her relationship with Blaze.

For the first time it occurred to her that she had left herself wide open to such speculation. Blaze had a wild reputation. Blaze was expected to scandalise and delight the locals with an unconventional lifestyle. In her teens, ninety per-cent of the juicy gossip on the grapevine had been devoted to Blaze and his sex life.

She was stunned by the sudden realisation that coincidence had undoubtedly lent some colour to the idea that Blaze was Rosie's father. Just over three years ago, she had suddenly left the area. She had chosen a teacher-training course in London because she had wanted to be with her mother. But didn't unmarried girls occasionally disappear when they didn't want people to know that they were pregnant? And ironically the dates would fit... In fact, had she slept with Blaze that long-ago night, Rosie's arrival eight and a bit months later would have dovetailed perfectly with an event that had never happened. And now here she was, back with a toddler in tow, living under Blaze's roof. Her skin heated. Dear heaven, no wonder folk were talking! Just how secure would her employment be when Blaze heard that same talk?

'You're not staying here with him!' Jim Hamilton bit out, clamping a rough hand to her narrow waist. 'He's trying to make a bloody fool of me——'

'But you manage that so well without any assistance,' a lazy drawl, laden with contemptuous amusement, slotted in smoothly.

Shattered by such naked provocation, Chrissy whirled round. Blaze cast her a glittering smile. Lounging in a doorway, he emanated an aura of astounding cool. With a bull-like snort, her father thrust her bodily aside and headed for Blaze instead.

Leaping back to life, Chrissy darted between the two men. Knowing how violent her father's temper could be, she was afraid he would take a swing at Blaze if she didn't intervene.

'Get out of the way!' Jim Hamilton raged. 'Let me at him!'

'I don't need your protection, Chrissy,' Blaze murmured drily.

'She's coming home. *You* can keep the brat!' her father told him.

'I'm staying h-here.' Cringing with embarrassment, Chrissy none the less had the strength to stand her ground. Her father was a bully, ready to seize on the first sign of weakness. 'I can't stop you thinking what you do, b-but I want to tell you that not a word of it is true.'

'Don't waste your breath, sweetheart,' Blaze advised, tugging her backwards into sudden disturbingly intimate contact with his hard, muscled length. He linked both arms in a blatant statement of possession round her slight, trembling body. Chrissy's eyes widened to their fullest extent and she went rigid, wondering what on earth he was playing at.

Almost tipped over the edge by the sight of such intimacy, Jim Hamilton swore viciously, the veins knotting warningly in his forehead. 'He was with Elaine in London!' he suddenly roared at her. 'He dropped her back on the doorstep this morning! Does that give you something to think about, you stupid——!'

'London...E-Elaine?' Chrissy parroted, with a gasp of disbelief, twisting her head to stare up at Blaze in astonished query. 'You w-were w-with E-Elaine?'

Drawing back a step, Jim Hamilton angled a triumphant smirk at Blaze. Chrissy's heartbeat was thumping so loudly in her eardrums that she felt faint and sick. Blaze wasn't looking at her. He wasn't denying the accusation either. Her throat closed over. Shock was reverbating through her in waves. All of a sudden her father was the least of her worries. So intense was her self-absorption that she turned again to Blaze, almost pleadingly this time, willing him with every fibre of her body to tell her that it wasn't true.

He couldn't have been with Elaine...he simply couldn't have been! Scant hours ago, Blaze had been telling her that it was *her* he wanted. He hated Elaine...he had to hate Elaine for what she had done! Indifferent to her father's presence, she attempted to repeat that unanswered question. 'You w-w-were w-w-w——' She stammered hopelessly, unable to get the words out this time, so great was her distress.

Her father's face twisted with revulsion. Her speech impediment had always affected him that way. 'What man would want to live with you spluttering and stuttering like an imbecile when he could have Elaine?' he demanded derisively.

Blaze hit him. He flattened her back against the wall and moved so fast that it was over before she even knew what was happening. Jim Hamilton went flying backwards, and, before he could pick himself up, a hand like a hoist anchored to his collar and he was all but thrown out of the front door.

'You put a foot within a hundred yards of Chrissy again and you're dead, Hamilton! I'll destroy you,' she heard Blaze promise in a chillingly icy drawl. 'Elaine will be the least of your problems.'

Chrissy was shivering. She hugged her arms clumsily round herself. She felt as if she was inside a glass bubble and everything else was happening outside it. She just couldn't react. The bombshell her father had unleashed had devastated her, and on one level she was striving to comprehend why she was in such agony. So he was seeing Elaine ... so what? she tried to tell herself.

Elaine was everything she herself was not. Elaine was very beautiful, very witty and entertaining when she wanted to be and no doubt very sexy as well. But what Chrissy couldn't understand was why he hadn't just told her and why he had been playing that game with her today in the Pheasant. For it must have been a game, the pretence that he found *her* desirable. She hurt all over. Her skin hurt. Her bones hurt. She had never been in such pain.

'You bottomed out badly in the parent lottery, didn't you?' Blaze murmured smoothly, strolling gracefully down the hall towards her, putting out enough electric energy to electrocute the unwary. Blaze, she registered sickly, had been exhilarated by that ghastly scene with her father. He had actually *enjoyed* the confrontation. 'Relax; he won't be back. He's too much of a coward. Bloody hell, you're terrified of him, aren't you?

She wasn't. Her father was loud, uncouth and frequently cruel, but she had never been afraid of him. She was the least favoured child, with no outstanding talents which might have made him proud of her. He had a handsome son and a beautiful daughter and would have been quite content had his family ended there. Once Chrissy had been labelled a disappointment she had been ignored. It had been her defection to her mother's side that had turned her father's indifference to outright dislike.

No, she wasn't terrified of her father. The only individual capable of terrifying her was right in front of her now, the rapacious smile of a tiger on his darkly handsome face.

'Come on.' He prised her carefully away from the wall and pressed her down on a sofa in the sitting-room. 'You're not involved in any of this. Don't let it worry you. I wouldn't hurt you. Why would I want to?' he asked softly, soothingly, much the same way as she had heard him calm a frightened horse.

He was crouched down in front of her. She was nailed in place by the full force of sapphire eyes that controlled and commanded. She felt like a butterfly on the end of a pin, but somehow she still couldn't drag her disobedient gaze from him. He lifted a cool hand and brushed an almost teasing forefinger along the tremulous line of her mouth. 'You can speak to me. I don't mind the stammer. In fact, I think it's kind of cute. It doesn't bother *me* at all.'

Incredulously she registered that he thought that was why she wasn't talking. But what chilled her most of all was the awareness that this was a male one hundred per cent confident of a sympathetic reception, a male utterly and absolutely convinced that nothing she had heard, nothing she had learnt, was likely to antagonise her.

'Chrissy...' He sighed. 'So I intend to get even—why should that bother you? Your father treats you like dirt, your sister treats you like trash, and you were ready to starve sooner than ask them for help. We are not talking about a close-knit family unit here.'

'"Getting even",' she echoed jerkily. 'And I'm part of it. Th-that's why you gave me this job...'

'Did I accidentally nearly run over you on purpose?' he mocked. 'I won't deny that I foresaw your father's reaction to your presence under my roof. It amused me, but that wasn't the sole reason. You were in dire straits and I was in a position to help you. It suited me to hire you and I wouldn't have done it if there hadn't been a job for you.'

'I came too cheap.' Tearing free of his mesmeric gaze, she studied her linked hands. 'You've been using me——'

'How? All I did was give you a job.'

He had suggested a familiarity that didn't exist between them when he'd put his arms round her. He had done that, she saw now, for her father's benefit. In the same way, he had employed her. Furthermore, he wouldn't be at all concerned by local gossip, not when that same gossip was seen as a humiliation by her father. She saw it all now and she felt stone-cold as she tasted the extent of her own blind stupidity.

Everything had been planned. The stable girl finding her in his bed the first morning. The hot embrace up at the jumps. The trip to the Pheasant today, seemingly so spontaneous and thoughtful. Her cheeks burned hot as hellfire. No, nobody within a hundred-mile radius of the local grapevine could now be suffering from the slightest doubt that her relationship with Blaze was of an exceedingly intimate nature. Blaze had made damn sure of that! Her reputation had been most thoroughly dragged in the mire.

And the irony of it all was that only the enemy had sought to warn her off! Hamish had been speaking the absolute truth when he'd said that Blaze was a total bastard. And yet that was something she had always known... Just when had she first begun to let that awareness slip? When he'd rescued them from desperation and given her a job? Or when he'd touched her and it had been like every fantasy she had ever had all presented in one unbearably tempting and fascinating package?

'Chrissy...'

A shudder disturbed her rigidity. She wanted to throw herself at him, kicking and screaming. She wanted to hurt him the way he had hurt her. But that wasn't within her power. It had all been a game for him, and she was just a pawn on his board, not an important playing piece. She wanted to make some wildly dramatic gesture to punish him, but that too was beyond her reach. She couldn't just walk out. She had no money, nowhere to go, and Rosie to consider. In any case, she had already played her role for Blaze unknowingly. As far as her father was concerned, she was deliberately and shamelessly flaunting her promiscuity with his biggest enemy. Had she had any relationship worth saving with her father, it had just been destroyed for good. And much Blaze would care about that!

'And what h-have you planned for my sister?' she heard herself prompt in a taut undertone from which all emotion had been wiped.

He was standing by the oak dresser, pouring himself a glass of brandy from an exquisite Georgian decanter. Firelight gleamed on his black hair, silhouetting his hard, classical profile, the aristocratic jut of his nose and the wide perfection of his mouth. A dark avenging angel, she saw with a shiver, untouched by mere human emotions. He would break Elaine, smash her into pieces. Elaine was an accident waiting to happen in Blaze's radius.

'My business...nothing whatsoever to do with you.' He cast her a nakedly perceptive glance, his lips twisting with grim amusement. 'And even if you warned her, she wouldn't believe you.'

Chrissy didn't trust herself to speak. But she knew that it was unlikely that her sister would listen to her. She also knew that she would still try to make Elaine listen. She had no intention of condoning or assisting Blaze with silence. Yet increasingly what dominated her racing thoughts was a morbid need to know exactly how far Blaze had gone in his desire for revenge. How often had he seen Elaine? Had he made love to her as well? Dear God, the imagery that leapt into her undisciplined mind knotted her stomach with nausea. And she surprised inside herself an emotion more shameful and humiliating than anything she had yet experienced.

It was jealousy, bitter as bile in her shaken system, burning up through the steadily widening cracks in her composure. The discovery devastated her. That she could feel such a thing after all she had learnt was disgusting, hateful, utterly shameful!

'I'm going out.' The keys of the Ferrari were clasped in one lean hand.

Chrissy jerked upright. 'To see Elaine?' The instant the question escaped her, she bitterly regretted it.

'When I give you the right to query my every move I'll let you know,' Blaze drawled softly. 'And at this moment in time all we have is a somewhat unconventional working relationship. Beyond that? *Nada* . . .'

Nothing, she translated. He didn't need to string her along any more. She had played her part well. He hadn't even had to go to the boring lengths of actually making love to her to extract her best performance from her. She climbed the stairs like an old lady and then suddenly, without the smallest warning, she was having to run to the bathroom to be horribly and thoroughly sick.

Afterwards, she splashed her face with shaking hands. *Nada* . . . nothing. His sudden, lancing cruelty had been like a whiplash on already raw flesh. She felt absolutely

HERE'S HOW TO PLAY
"MATCH 3"

1 Detach this, your "MATCH 3" Game, & the page of stamps enclosed. Look for matching symbols among the stamps & stick all you find on your "MATCH 3" Game.

2 Successfully complete rows 1 through 3 & you will instantly & automatically qualify for a chance to win a Big Money Prize—up to a MILLION-$$$ in Lifetime Income ($33,333.33 each year for 30 years). (SEE BACK OF BOOK FOR DETAILS.)

3 Successfully complete row 4 & we will send you 4 brand-new HARLEQUIN PRESENTS® novels—for FREE! These Free Books have a cover price of $3.25 each, but they are yours to keep absolutely free. There's no catch. You're under no obligation to buy anything. We charge nothing—ZERO—for your first shipment. And you don't have to make any minimum number of purchases—not even one!

4 The fact is, thousands of Readers enjoy receiving books by mail from the Harlequin Reader Service®. They like the convenience of home delivery...they like getting the best new novels months before they're available in stores...and they love our discount prices!

5 Successfully complete row 5 &, in addition to the Free Books, we will also send you a very nice Free Surprise Gift, as extra thanks for trying our Reader Service.

6 Play the "Lucky Stars" & "Lucky Keys" Games also enclosed & you could WIN AGAIN & AGAIN because these are Bonus Prizes, all for one winner, & on top of any Cash Prize you may win!

YES! I've completed my "MATCH 3" Game. Send me any Big Money Prize to which I am entitled just as soon as winners are determined. Also send me the Free Books & Free Surprise Gift under the no-obligation-to-buy-ever terms explained above and on the back of the stamps & reply. (No purchase necessary as explained below.) 106 CIH AWG2
(U-NP-05/95)

Name

Street Address   Apt. #

City   State   Zip Code
©1991 HARLEQUIN ENTERPRISES LTD.

humiliated. Bruised, beaten, an object of scorn. And beyond that was this overpowering inner pain that told her that the cut had gone deeper still than he knew or she could ever have dreamt in her worst nightmares.

CHAPTER SIX

CHRISSY parked behind Elaine's Porsche. Her father rarely bothered to use the garages, and the fact that there was no other car visible led her to hope that he had already left for his office in Reading. She had left Rosie with Floss, telling her that she had some shopping to do. Floss had remarked on her pallor but not on her reddened eyes. Floss, she suspected, saw far more than she ever betrayed.

Blaze had eaten breakfast with inhuman cool, even chatting to Rosie in between times. Chrissy hadn't been able to eat a thing. Food would have choked her. She had lain awake throughout the long night, torturing herself with self-loathing, desperate for an avenue of escape that would take her far from Westleigh Hall. She didn't want to be anywhere near Blaze. She didn't ever want to see him again. But escape required money she didn't have. She was horrified by the trap in which she found herself.

Elaine, clad in an expensive black lace négligé set, opened the door. 'What do you want?' she demanded.

'May I come in?' Chrissy asked tautly.

'Suit yourself!' Walking into the lounge, Elaine left her to follow.

'I'm surprised you're still here,' Chrissy admitted. 'I thought Dad might have thrown you out when he realised that you were seeing B-Blaze.' Helplessly, she stumbled over his name, her strained mouth tightening.

'Oh, I told Dad; he just gave me a lift home...and that was all,' Elaine told her smugly. 'He always believes what I tell him. I gather you weren't so successful.'

'Meaning?'

'Don't play dumb, Chrissy. I know you're working for Blaze. He told me when we were in London...'

'When we were in London'... The careless intimacy of the admission twisted Chrissy's stomach. The assurance also told her that Blaze had left nothing to chance. 'Did you run into him a-accidentally?' She despised herself for asking.

Elaine raised a tart brow. 'Don't be more stupid than you can help... and, if I were you, I'd start looking around for another job. Blaze always did have a weird sense of humour, but when I move in you move out. Nobody's going to be cracking three-in-a-bed jokes behind my back!'

'You're moving in?' Chrissy looked incredulous.

'Naturally... when the place is more habitable. Blaze knows I'm not the type to rough it.' Elaine studied her reflection intently in the mirror above the fireplace, flicked a silver-blonde strand of hair back in place, and gave herself a fat, cat-got-the-cream smile of satisfaction. 'Once I explained my side of that stupid business with the old man, we were back where we were three years ago.'

'Really?'

'Yes, really.' Elaine swung round. 'I had no idea what Dad was planning to do.'

'Rubbish.'

'Blaze understands... I don't give a damn whether you do or not!' Elaine said sharply. 'Lord Whitley agreed to the stakes. If he didn't have the money, he shouldn't have played. Nobody twisted his arm, for goodness' sake! And you know Dad—he doesn't let anyone owe him money. He had a right to try and collect it. He won it fair and square. It wasn't our fault that the old boy had a dodgy ticker. He wasn't going to last forever anyway!'

The ease with which Elaine exonerated herself from all responsibility shook Chrissy. Her sister's conscience was clearly at peace. Evidently Blaze had pretended to accept her wholly selfish explanation and that would be enough for Elaine, who was too self-absorbed to be sensitive.

Chrissy took a deep breath. 'I want you to listen to me——'

'About what?' Elaine looked crashingly bored. 'You didn't need to come here to tell me that there's nothing going on between you and Blaze. My God!' With a derisive laugh, she surveyed her kid sister. 'As if he'd ever be that desperate!'

Chrissy went white. Although it was the truth, it still hurt to be taunted. 'Elaine, Blaze blames you for his grandfather's death. Whatever else he's telling you, he's lying. He couldn't possibly be planning any future that includes you——'

'Oh, for heaven's sake!' Elaine groaned.

'He wants revenge. He hasn't forgotten what you did . . .'

'You're jealous, aren't you?'

'I'm trying to warn you——'

'Where the hell do you think you get the right to talk to me like that about Blaze?' Elaine lost her temper suddenly. 'I'm not listening to it. See yourself out!'

Left talking to thin air, Chrissy followed her sister to her bedroom. 'I know you don't want to believe me, but why would I lie?'

'Because you're a jealous bitch!' Elaine condemned. 'Blaze is worth millions and you can't stand for me to get him!'

'Millions?' Chrissy queried drily.

'At least. His father left him the lot.' Elaine smiled to herself. 'A total fluke, but amazing good luck. His father married and had two legitimate kids, but the whole family went down in a plane crash eighteen months ago. Blaze copped the lot.'

She had lost her kid sister's attention. Chrissy was staring at the box protruding from the waste-paper bin. Unless she was very much mistaken . . . She bent and fished it out. She hadn't been mistaken. It belonged to a pregnancy-testing kit!

'Oh, hell!' Registering the source of her stillness, Elaine snatched the evidence angrily from her and thrust it back in the bin. 'I'm warning you...if you don't keep your mouth shut, I'll kill you! I've got a booking at a clinic next week and that will take care of that!'

Chrissy was stunned. 'You're pregnant?'

'Fabulous timing, don't you think?' Elaine muttered sulkily. 'I could scream! All my own doing, of course. I let Steve persuade me just that once and look where I am now!'

'And you're planning to have an abortion?' Chrissy was deeply disturbed by the announcement. 'You c-can't do that, Elaine. Not for Blaze's benefit.'

'Who else would I do it for? Stop looking at me like that!' Elaine told her furiously. 'It's my choice, my decision...'

'But presumably you wanted the baby when it was conceived,' reasoned Chrissy, appalled by her sister's intentions towards her unborn child.

'Times change. I want a quick, clean divorce so that Blaze can marry me and I'm not complicating the issue.'

'Has Blaze mentioned marriage?' Chrissy breathed.

'Not yet...but he will,' Elaine stated with her usual confidence. 'So you must see how impossible it would be for me to be pregnant with another man's child.'

Chrissy sank down shakily on the edge of the bed. Dear heaven, but Elaine could be callous. She wanted Blaze, and nothing, not even the precious gift of life in her womb, was to be allowed to come before that ambition. If Steve ever found out, it would destroy him. But, worst of all, Elaine would be disposing of her unborn child for nothing, taking life for no good reason. How could she stand by and let that happen when she knew that Blaze was acting solely out of malice? No way did Blaze intend any future with her sister!

'If you're thinking of telling Blaze, I'll just deny it!' Elaine slammed at her. 'And he wouldn't care even if he did believe you!'

Since that was Chrissy's estimation as well, she bowed her head. Her brain was seething. What could she do to convince her sister that Blaze was deliberately leading her up the garden path? She simply couldn't stand by and allow Elaine to abort her baby, her own unborn nephew or niece, for Blaze's benefit. She wouldn't be able to live with herself if she did. Whatever decision Elaine reached in the near future, she must make that very serious decision without the false premise that Blaze would be in the picture.

Elaine vented a scornful laugh. 'I wonder if he's heard those utterly ridiculous rumours that he's the father of *your* child? I nearly asked him. Only Dad could be dumb enough to think that Blaze would ever have slept with you... I mean, when and where and how? But then Dad thinks no woman between fifteen and fifty is safe with Blaze!'

As inspiration took hold of her, Chrissy tensed. Suddenly she grasped that there was one way of dividing Elaine from Blaze. If she could convince her sister that that utterly ridiculous rumour *was* true...! Elaine would be outraged. Snatching up her bag, Chrissy dug into her purse to extract a photo of Rosie.

'When?' she repeated, tilting up her chin with determination. 'W-well, it was the night before your wedding. Blaze had crashed his car on the back lane of the Manor. He was very drunk and I took him home...'

Elaine's blue eyes fixed on her in disbelief. 'You're not being funny...'

'I w-wasn't trying to be.'

'I'm not going to listen to fairy-tales!' Elaine's voice had risen an octave, revealing that she was indeed listening.

'This is Rosie.' Chrissy cast the photo down on the bedspread almost carelessly, afraid to overplay her hand,

and then went on to tell Elaine in greater detail about
how she had come upon Blaze that night.

'He did crash his car... On the way to the church I
saw it being towed to the garage.' Elaine was staring down
at the photo, suddenly very pale and rigid. 'But he
wouldn't have slept with you! My God, you were barely
out of school!'

'Do you remember how weepy I was on your wedding
day?' Chrissy reminded her. 'I h-had a crush on him...
H-he was drunk and w-when he made a pass at me...
well, I was... I was flattered——'

'I won't believe it...I won't!' In sudden temper, Elaine
snatched the photo up and tore it violently in two.

'When I f-found out I was pregnant, I was devastated,
but I was down in London and I knew *he* wasn't likely
to be interested,' Chrissy continued, and her voice was
tremulous. On one level she couldn't believe that she
was doing this, telling this outrageous lie with all the
trimmings, but on another she knew that it was her only
hope of protecting Elaine's unborn child. 'I love kids,
you know that. That's w-why I had her. I r-reckoned it
was the only part of him I was ever likely to have...'

Inwardly, she cringed from that final fatuous assertion.

'It isn't true!' Elaine shrieked at her. 'You're making
it up!'

'Well, you ask yourself w-why he gave me this job,'
Chrissy dared with growing confidence. 'And while you
ponder that, s-spare a thought to what we were doing
in the Pheasant yesterday all afternoon.' Her cheeks
burned as she made that provocative suggestion.

The silence seethed.

'You——!' Words seemed to fail her sister. And
then suddenly she attacked, landing Chrissy such a slap
across the face that she almost knocked her off the bed.
'The only man I ever wanted! You, of all people!
It's revolting!'

Her cheek burning fierily, Chrissy hurriedly moved out of reach. Elaine was screeching at the top of her voice, 'Get out! I'll never forgive you for this...never!'

As she made it out to the hall, Elaine screamed after her, 'He was mine...do you hear me? He was mine!'

At least she was talking in the past tense. But then Elaine couldn't bear the idea that she had been sharing Blaze with her kid sister any more than she would be able to bear the knowledge that Blaze had been deceiving her. Chrissy should have felt guilty on Blaze's behalf but she didn't. He would never know what she had done. Elaine would go home to Steve. Elaine always ran for security when things got messy.

Chrissy drove to Reading, determined to give Blaze no opportunity to suspect that she had been anywhere near Elaine. On her return, Hamish answered the door at the Lodge. Floss had taken Rosie visiting in the village.

Floss had also left an elaborate salad in the fridge for Blaze's lunch. Even though it was after three, it was still there. Chrissy began pushing the furniture back into place in the drawing-room. Everything was sparkling. The professional cleaners, who had arrived before she went out, had, at her request, concentrated on the completed downstairs rooms. Of course, the decorators hadn't even begun yet. Every wall was crying out for paint and paper, but she was able to spread a particularly beautiful Persian rug on the polished mahogany floor of the drawing-room and, even without curtains, the room immediately began to take on a welcoming aspect. She was just thinking that tomorrow she would start trying to sort out the dining-room when she heard the Ferrari brake to a tyre-squealing halt outside.

A frown-line divided her delicate brows. Tension began to crawl up her rigid spine. Abruptly, she decided to take evasive action, and headed for the kitchen. She was halfway out into the yard when a set of powerful fingers closed like a vice over her forearm.

'And where are you going?' Blaze enquired, and there was something strange about his voice, something she couldn't quite grasp but which none the less lunged her into sudden, instinctive panic.

'T-to pick up R-Rosie!'

'Floss isn't back yet.'

'Oh.' She still hadn't managed to look at him, but from the instant she had heard his car she had felt as though every lie she had told Elaine was tattooed on her forehead for him to see. She broke out in nervous perspiration. 'Would you like your lunch?'

'Look at me!' he demanded in a savage undertone. Her breath coming in audible snatches from her convulsed throat, she lifted her head. He didn't know his own strength. The lean fingers anchored to her arm were biting deep into her shrinking flesh.

Warily, she collided with sapphire-blue eyes and connected with the ferocious tension splintering from him. It sprang out at her from the prominence of his tautened bone-structure, the dark flush overlying his cheekbones, the thinned flatness of his set mouth. His raw, searching scrutiny, alight with furious condemnation and suspicion, flamed over her pale, drawn face. It was like being hit by lightning. Her stomach lurched and dropped to the soles of her feet.

'Elaine came over here this morning, half dressed, hysterical and raving like a madwoman,' Blaze spelt out in a murderously controlled tone that sent a shiver down her spine.

Her blood ran cold in her veins. She was shattered. It had never occurred to her that Elaine would confront him. Had her sister actually told him what she had claimed? Surely not... Had she been wrong to assume that Elaine had too much pride to lower herself to such a head-on clash? The fact that her arm was about to drop off from lack of circulation suggested that she had been more wrong in that assumption than she had ever been wrong about anything in her life. And, since such a development had not once crossed her mind when she'd impulsively decided to lie to her sister, she was paralysed by sheer shock, staring up at him wide-eyed and stricken by an attack of mortification deep enough to drown in.

'Y-you're h-hurting me,' she whispered shakily.

He released her arm. Automatically, she massaged the bruised member while she thought frantically. Dear God, what was she going to do now? Of course, he wouldn't believe her. Elaine had, he wouldn't, she told herself. But then, if he didn't believe her, he would be perfectly capable of convincing Elaine that she had been lying. And if that happened she would be back to square one. She was appalled by the realisation that she was stuck with the lie now that he was aware of her claim. She had only one advantage: he had no memory of that night! At least, if he had, he had yet to betray the fact.

'I don't believe it's true...you've got to be lying!' The accusation was flung at her in wrathful challenge.

He was in shock, an unusual condition for Blaze Kenyon. That reaffirmed her view that he recalled nothing of that long-ago night. All she really had to do was stall him long enough for Elaine to leave the area.

'One,' he itemised with raw bite, 'you were only seventeen. There is no way that, even in the state I was in, I would have touched you! Two...I have never, ever had unprotected sex, not even when I was a teenager! Three...why wouldn't you have told me? Why would you agree to work for me and even then only spill the beans to Elaine?'

He had her cornered by the back door. The handle was digging into her spine. Hot colour had flushed her complexion. He raised a not quite steady hand and drove his fingers roughly through his luxuriant black hair. He really was shaken up. She hadn't imagined that anything could penetrate that tough self-assurance and cynicism, but this had. Momentarily, guilt tore at her, and then she remembered Elaine's baby, his savage and admitted desire to take revenge. As soon as it was safe to do so, she would tell him the truth, but not before.

'Damn you!' he slung at her with raw frustration. 'If you don't start talking, I won't be responsible for what I do next!'

'What e-exactly do you want me to say?' she managed, intimidated by the violent anger vibrating from him.

'You're lying! It's a sordid fabrication from start to finish! That's what I want you to say,' he informed her.

Thinking fast, she forced herself to meet that glittering stare of expectancy. 'I don't have to justify myself. I d-didn't know Elaine would tell you . . . I never planned for you to know. If you had stayed away from my sister,' she dared valiantly, 'you never would have known . . .'

'Is that supposed to make me feel better?'

'I don't care how you feel.' Recalling how she had felt that night, she really didn't. 'But I wasn't g-going to let you wreck Elaine's life. Now, will you let me go?'

'Your attitude doesn't make sense. If I am Rosie's father . . . which is highly unlikely . . . but, if I am, you're behaving as though it's irrelevant!' he condemned.

He had one hand braced against the door-lintel, and she ducked under it to escape. He spun so fast that she got precisely three feet before he dragged her back with one powerful hand. This time he was careful not to hurt her, but Chrissy didn't appreciate being physically controlled. 'Let go of me!'

'Like hell I will!' He pulled her out of the kitchen, down the hall, and thrust her into the drawing-room. 'If it takes me the rest of the day, you are going to tell me the truth!

What cool Chrissy had contrived to maintain was dissipating fast. He kicked the door shut and leant back against it. 'So where did this miraculous conception take place?' he prompted in sardonic invitation.

She felt hot all over, wishing in desperation that she could have told any lie less intimate than one which alleged that she had wantonly fallen into his arms for a brief sexual encounter one night when he had been too drunk even to remember the event the next day! She studied the floor. 'Your b-bedroom at the Manor...'

The silence fairly sizzled.

'The night I crashed my car?'

'Yes...you were drunk——'

'I was not drunk!' Blaze countered in raw interruption. 'I was suffering from concussion and a particularly nasty bout of flu...'

'You had a whisky bottle with you in the woods.' Glancing up, she saw the flash of some no doubt dim recollection literally freeze his dark, taut features.

'I thought I just had a cold. I took a couple of drinks in the hope of feeling better, and then I think I threw the bottle away...'

'Yes,' she confirmed.

'So you saw me there. What happened next?'

'I tried to persuade you that you needed medical attention,' she continued tautly. 'Then I suggested I drive you back up to the Manor...'

'I was in a car. I remember that,' he conceded roughly.

'We had to go in through the courtyard...'

'Nothing that you have so far said confirms your story. I do accept that you saw that bedroom, though.' A flash of white teeth briefly showed in the grimmest of smiles. 'No wonder you got in such a state when I noticed the startling similarity between that bedroom and the one you created upstairs. How did we get as far as the bedroom?'

Her hands were shaking. She twisted them together. Dear heaven, how could she continue with this? It was an interrogation and one which would pull no punches, she sensed in consternation. 'I took you up there...'

'And why did you do that? Or is that a surpassingly stupid question?'

Her fair skin crimsoned. 'You were ill...you needed to lie down——'

'I could have lain down in any of the rooms down-stairs,' he cut in ruthlessly, 'so why go to the trouble of taking me upstairs?'

Was he actually trying to insinuate that she had somehow set him up? How dared he do that? Abruptly and in some astonishment she registered that she was actually reacting as though he had made love to her that night!

'It w-wasn't something I thought about, for goodness' sake! I was worried about y-you... you were in a state of collapse!' she protested.

'And then what?'

The horrible silence hummed and plucked at her nerves. She bit at her lower lip and averted her gaze from his. 'I was ringing the d-doctor and you pulled me a-away from the phone and... and you k-kissed me.'

'Really?' He sounded offensively sceptical.

And because that *was* the truth, she flung up her head furiously. 'Yes, I was p-pretty shocked too when it happened!'

His jawline squared. 'Continue.'

She took a deep breath and fought not to be squeamish. 'And then w-we... we did it,' she muttered in a near whisper.

'We did it,' he repeated with caustic bite. 'Your talent for invention becomes more extraordinary by the minute! You admit that I was in a state of collapse...'

Tension was tightening in a band of steel round her throbbing temples. 'Yes, but——'

'I barely knew you. You were just a kid!' he blistered back.

'I was n-nearly eighteen!' she stammered, suddenly covering her hot face with her hands and swinging away from him. In heaven's name, what had she let herself in for? Tears of emotional stress suddenly lashed her strained eyes.

'By my rating, you were still a child. Even in the state I was in, I don't believe I would have touched you!' he asserted fiercely.

She wasn't playing her part with sufficient conviction, she acknowledged, and if she didn't make a greater effort he was likely to drag the truth out of her. She forced her teeming mind to focus on that night. 'You w-were very upset about your grandfather... you called Elaine a t-tart... I didn't know why you were so angry...'

'Are you saying that I raped you?' he demanded.

'No!' Aghast, she swiftly denied the charge, and half turned from him, wiping the dampness from her cheeks with an unsteady hand.

'Then you're saying that I made love to you to get even with your father and your sister.'

The suggestion just hung there and she seized on it like a lifeline because it gave him the motive he seemed to need to accept any part of her story. 'I didn't know about the poker game... or any of it then...'

'And you're telling me that you just fell into my arms without a murmur?' he derided. 'You thought I was drunk. You admit I was angry, that I abused your sister to your face——'

'I w-wasn't thinking about what I was doing!' Her sudden interruption carried credibility. She hadn't had the discipline to think about anything when she was in his arms that night. 'It just happened!'

'But I don't remember it. And you would think that I would recall such a sudden and overwhelming attack of lust, wouldn't you?' he murmured silkily. 'I have only the sketchiest memory of that night. Parts of it are a complete blank, and you're playing on that.'

'I can't s-stop you thinking that,' she mumbled, her slight shoulders drooping with the strain of the pro-longed tension.

'So then you can fill in the blanks. How did we... to borrow that schoolgirlish phrase..."do it"?'

Chrissy blenched and shot him a helpless look of dismay.

'I want details,' he informed her unashamedly.

'You have no right to try and h-humiliate me!' she gasped.

'I think I have every right when you consider the seriousness of a paternity charge.' Brilliantly blue eyes scorched hers in scalding challenge. 'DNA tests can't be done overnight, I'm afraid.'

Chrissy turned even paler. He was talking about bringing the law and the medical profession into it. She calmed her fears by reminding herself that within days she would no longer be required to maintain the lie. Then, she guessed, she and Rosie would certainly be out on the street again. Dear lord, she wondered if she would have begun this had she known how far it would lead.

'Naturally, it would be more sensible if we settled this here and now,' Blaze pointed out insidiously. 'After all, you can't hope to fool a DNA test, and if this is just some very stupid attempt to keep me away from Elaine I'm willing to forgive and forget if you tell me the truth now. I won't fire you. This hasn't yet gone any further than the three of us.'

The expectant silence drummed fingers of dread on her nerve-strings. He was offering her a clean escape, the promise of a complete pardon. And she wanted to take it. That one outrageous lie had escalated into a giant black cloud, weighing her down. It had turned into something much bigger and much more serious than she could ever have dreamt. But then she remembered Elaine's baby and she grimly accepted the need to sustain the lie a little longer.

She trawled her imagination for the kind of details that might at least deflect him from the most intimate questions. Walking jerkily over to the window, she breathed in deep. 'We... we m-made love on the... on the floor. It d-didn't last very long.' Her cheeks were so hot that she felt sunburnt. 'You didn't take your clothes off. Then...then you told me to g-get out and I went home. Is there anything else you want to know?' she mumbled.

The silence stretched and hummed. Then she heard him breathe in deeply.

'I don't think I want to know any of this,' he admitted tightly.

He would strangle her when he found out that she had been lying! But he sounded quieter, and that relieved her. She really didn't think she could stand the interrogation much longer without making a slip.

'And when did you find out you were pregnant?'

She flinched. 'I was already in London.'

'You were with your mother—why didn't she insist that you contact me?'

'I w-wouldn't tell her who the father was.'

'But what about the social services?' he shot at her without warning. 'I understand that they now insist on knowing the father's name and serving him with a maintenance order for support of the child.'

In alarm, she said, 'But I never made a claim. I n-never asked for help!'

Blaze looked balked of his prey. He was pacing the floor like a tiger marking out his imprisonment in a cage, his agile brain seeking to pin down the weaknesses in her story. A sliver of shameful satisfaction darted through Chrissy. At least while he was here he wasn't with Elaine. And part of her was beginning to believe that a few days of hell were his just deserts for the unforgivable way he had sought to use her. She loathed and despised him, she told herself, her small hands closing into fists. He had set her up and used her without conscience, and he would have got off scot-free if she hadn't learnt that Elaine was planning to have an abortion.

'How have you lived, then?' he demanded abruptly.

'I sold off Mum's jewellery bit by bit...'

He swore viciously, restive as a predatory cat on hot bricks. He was pale beneath his bronzed skin, and lines of strain grooved between his mouth and nose.

It was time to let him off the hook, figuratively speaking, Chrissy decided. Maybe then he would calm down. 'You were never intended to know about th-this. It's just something that happened and it's all behind me now,' she stressed. 'I'd just as soon you forgot it again...'

He stopped dead, angling a blazing look of incredulity at her. 'Forget it again? How the hell could I forget it? You're telling me that I took advantage of one of the most naïve teenagers I had ever met in some sordid grappling session that by your account doesn't even deserve the dignity of being deemed a one-night stand...and you ask me to forget it?' he roared at her. 'Tell me just how I am supposed to forget that you are accusing me of being Rosie's father.'

'I didn't accuse you of being anything,' she reminded him fearfully.

'And your unbelievably martyred silence in circumstances that would have taxed the temperament of a saint... I'm supposed to be grateful for that?' Blaze lashed back at her contemptuously. 'You let me give you a job! You never by the smallest word or gesture even hinted that Rosie might be mine! Give me a break! This is not some soap opera—this is real life. Why did you tell me that Rosie's father was in prison?'

Her breath caught in her throat. She swallowed hard, thought fast. 'I was afraid you'd suspect the truth. I w-wanted to put you off the track——'

'But I was never on the bloody track to begin with! You must have realised that I didn't remember that night?'

Chrissy was shaking like a leaf in a high wind, no longer able to withstand his attacks. 'I...I was only certain of th-that later——'

Blaze cut ruthlessly in on her yet again. 'You told me that you thought you were in love with Rosie's father!

How the hell could you have thought you were in love with me? I'd only spoken to you half a dozen times in my life before that night, and you used to look at me then as if I were something the cat brought in!' he informed her rawly.

She burst into floods of tears and ran out of the room. Had she withstood that continuous barrage one second longer, she would have broken down and confessed the truth. She leant back against her bedroom door, her heartbeat threatening to burst from her chest as she strained to hear any sound of pursuit. When the silence continued, she slumped.

CHAPTER SEVEN

WITH a bitten-back gasp of effort, Chrissy heaved the second case into the Land Rover. She was literally shaking with nerves. It was so quiet that she could hear the footsteps of the security man patrolling the well-lit yard behind the house. Blaze took no risks with the extremely valuable horses he trained.

She hurried back into the house. They had to leave now. There was no other choice. All she was really doing was protecting herself from any further unpleasantness. Herself and Rosie, she reminded herself. When she had pulled herself together, she had come downstairs and gone to collect Rosie. She had started to make dinner, miserably acknowledging that the practicalities of life continued even in the midst of crisis. Only then a virtual bombshell had exploded beneath her naïve feet.

Looking out of the kitchen window, she had seen an executive type crossing the yard to greet Blaze. And she had recognised him with a sinking sensation in the pit of her stomach. After all, she had met him once... very briefly. His name was Guy and he was Blaze's lawyer. As the two men had come through the rear hall that led into the kitchen, she had heard Guy say mockingly, 'So tell me, what's so damned private you refuse to discuss it on the phone?'

She had dived into the walk-in larder sooner than see Blaze, but Rosie must have tried to intercept him. 'Not now, Rosie!' he had grated with a ferocity he had never before angled at her little sister.

Rosie had promptly burst into floods of uncomprehending tears, and over the racket Blaze had raked, 'I don't want dinner, Chrissy!' making a nonsense of her attempt to conceal herself in the larder.

He had been closeted with Guy in the drawing-room for over two hours. Then she had heard the Ferrari starting up. As soon as she'd heard that, she had sped upstairs to pack, determined to be gone before Blaze returned. The speed with which he had resorted to his lawyer had shattered her, and his rejection of Rosie had brought home to her another aspect of the situation which she should have foreseen. There was absolutely no way that they could remain under this roof another night.

For all she knew, it was a criminal act to make the sort of claim she had made. He could probably take her to court for defamation of character or some such thing. The sight of Guy with his executive case had petrified Chrissy!

It was unfortunate that she had had to put Rosie to bed while she waited and prayed for Blaze to go out. Dear God, was he likely to pursue her for disappearing with the remainder of the housekeeping money? It was the only money she had. It would get them on a train to somewhere, anywhere. They would have to spend the night in the car, and before she got on the train she would phone to say where she had left it in case Blaze thought she had stolen that as well.

Pulling back the blankets, Chrissy lifted Rosie. She had put her to bed in all her clothes. Her heartbeat thumping in her eardrums, she started down the stairs again. She was halfway to the Land Rover when someone stepped out of the shadows of the vast overgrown shrubbery to the far side of the house.

Her breath escaped in a sudden hiss of fright. Blaze strolled forward into the path of light spilling from the hall. Very tall, very dark and very, very angry. The anger was like a physical force, focused on her with terrifying intensity. For the longest moment of her life, Blaze stared at her standing there, awkwardly cradling Rosie, who was growing heavier by the minute. Chrissy turned red and then white.

'Give me the car keys!' he bit out harshly.

'They're on the d-dashboard,' she stammered.

Silently, he retrieved them and strode round to unlock the boot. 'If there are cases in here, I'll have her made a ward of court!'

Their cases were revealed like a statement of guilty intent. Under the onslaught of a seething sapphire glance, Chrissy studied the ground instead. She heard the crash as the cases were dumped back into the hall. A second later, Rosie was virtually snatched from her arms.

Shaking off her nervous paralysis, Chrissy followed him up the stairs.

Blaze laid her sister gently back down on her bed. 'Take her clothes off and tuck her in,' he instructed in an icy undertone.

With clumsy, uncertain hands, Chrissy stripped Rosie down to her underwear and pulled the covers back over her. Throughout, she was unbearably conscious of Blaze's simmering presence. A ward of court? What on earth was he talking about? Damn him, he must have parked the Ferrari behind the stable block. That was why she hadn't heard the car. Seeing the front door wide and the Discovery sitting with two doors hinged open, he had backed off to see what was going to happen next.

'Bolting runs in the Hamilton genes, I gather,' Blaze drawled with contempt.

Her cheeks flamed at the reference to her mother's moonlit flit from her father.

Lean brown fingers enclosed her narrow wrist as he trailed her downstairs. 'If you take the car out at all, you leave Rosie behind from now on,' he told her. 'You don't take her off this estate. One wrong move, sweetheart, and I go to court for custody. Do you understand? Or do you want that in writing?'

Custody? Taut as a bowstring, Chrissy hovered in the centre of the rug in the drawing-room. The tip of her tongue snaked out to moisten her dry lips. 'I——'

'Where the hell did you think you were taking her? Back to some backstreet slum where I couldn't find you? Your next miscalculation will be your last,' he asserted, making a shiver of fear run down her spine.

Her lashes were fluttering in bewilderment, and then, suddenly, she understood. Blaze believed her. He believed that Rosie was his child. She was shattered by the acknowledgement. Had anyone asked her, she would have said that Blaze would still be denying paternity a month from now by every means within his power. She had assumed that he was drumming up the big guns when he so swiftly consulted his lawyer, and evidently he had been ... only he wasn't intending to aim those guns in the direction she had expected.

'I thought you d-didn't believe me...' she began, willing him to start disbelieving her again. This was an even more alarming development than the last. And she was fresh out of inspiration.

'If I had one shred of doubt left, it vanished when I saw you making a break for it!' he shot at her wrathfully.

'But why?

'You told Elaine in the first instance, not me. You didn't want me to know. You made no demands and, at the first opportunity, you try to bolt. If you were on the make, none of it would have happened that way,' he asserted with cold cynicism.

'I could still be l-lying,' she heard herself say, and wondered if there was insanity in her genes as well as bolting, because now she was striving to rouse his doubts again. 'I thought that leaving was the best thing I could do——'

'Where were you going?' he demanded again.

'I was going to get on a train...'

'Where?'

'I hadn't d-decided!' she gasped.

'What the hell sort of a mother are you?' Blaze blistered at her without warning. 'Don't Rosie's needs deserve some consideration? What about her rights? You drag her out of bed in the middle of the night and you don't even know where you're taking her! How much money have you got?'

Chrissy stood there mute, fighting back tears of mingled rage and guilt.

'I want an answer,' Blaze grated.

'About fifty pounds... It's yours!' she muttered fiercely. 'I was stealing it!'

'Fifty quid! Is that all?' he breathed incredulously. 'You're not any more fit to be out there on your own than Rosie is! How far did you think you were going to get on that?'

'I just wanted to g-get away from *you*!'

'Like hell you do!' he derided, running a scathingly disbelieving scrutiny over her small, slight figure. 'Something spooked you into the great escape, but it wasn't a genuine desire to get away from me. No way, José.'

Fury sparked in her defiant gaze. 'Where do you get that idea?'

'Right now, we have more important things to discuss,' he spelt out, his expressive mouth twisting with impatience. 'Why don't you sit down so that we can talk about this calmly?'

'Maybe I d-don't want to sit down!' Chrissy slung back at him.

'Don't be so damned childish!' He closed the gap between them in one long stride, clamped his hands round her slim waist, and dumped her into the wing armchair behind her. 'Now co-operate,' he instructed grimly. 'I want to see Rosie's birth certificate.'

'You can't,' she told him.

'Why the hell not?'

Belle had torn it up in a rage one day and Chrissy had never got around to getting a copy. 'It got lost in one of the moves... I never applied for a r-replacement.'

He swore. 'Am I named as her father?'

She shook her head.

He actually looked annoyed, sapphire eyes hardening as they rested on her. 'When is her birthday?'

Reluctantly, she divulged the date.

He frowned. 'She was premature, then...'

'Only by a couple of weeks.' In fact, Belle had been ten days past her due date when she finally went into labour.

'Where was she born?'

She named the hospital.

'Most women in the same position would have opted for an abortion...'

'Belle had religious objections,' Chrissy filled in before she realised her slip.

'And she persuaded you to go ahead with the pregnancy?'

He had misunderstood. Hurriedly, she nodded agreement.

'Did you have a rough time having her?' he demanded abruptly.

It took her several seconds to understand what he was talking about. He was actually asking her what sort of birth experience she had had. Her pale skin flamed. Now she really knew how a woman living a nightmare of her own making felt. 'Look, I d-don't want to discuss that kind of thing with you!'

His striking bone-structure hardened. 'It's a pity you weren't so fastidious when I allegedly flattened you to the floor three years ago,' he murmured smoothly. 'Then you just might have said no and we wouldn't be in this predicament now!'

'Well, I l-like that——' she began furiously.

'Evidently you must have done but it's hardly some-thing to boast about,' he continued harshly. 'I have never treated a woman that crudely in my life!'

Clearly the fanciful sex scene she had created for his benefit had damaged his all-male ego. Chrissy was de-lighted...in fact she couldn't have been more pleased

that she had accidentally hit on a description that he
found offensive. 'No? You surprise me!'

He reached down slowly and drew her up out of the
chair. What shook her was that she instinctively let
herself be drawn. 'No,' he repeated very quietly, slowly
winding his fingers into the tumbling strands of hair lying
against her breast to anchor her in place.

His thumb brushed against her breast, and instantly
all the oxygen in her lungs was sucked dry by the sudden
shocked release of her breath. Beneath the thin T-shirt,
her sensitive flesh swelled and her nipple peaked into a
tight bud of response. Involuntarily her eyes closed and
she swayed. His thumb rubbed against the hardened nub
he had teased into visibility and a deep, unbearably sharp
pang of response stirred low in her stomach and made
her ache.

'If you responded like this then,' Blaze murmured
thickly, 'even the kitchen table could begin to look as
inviting as a feather bed.'

As she was wrenched from the drowning sensuality
that had plunged her into shameless oblivion, her eyes
flew open, but it was too late; Blaze had closed both
arms round her and she collided with dark dense blue
before his mouth came crashing down hard on hers. Her
feet left the floor in the midst of that devouring kiss and
he tumbled her down on the sofa without breaking the
connection.

The sofa was like a rock. It hurt her shoulder-blades.
She didn't care. That was an irrelevance in comparison
to the welter of other sensations controlling her. He
brought his full weight down on her, mouth to mouth,
chest to breast, thigh to thigh, until not an inch of her
was not connected to some part of him and at every
point of connection she burned in varying degrees. His
tongue was stabbing into the moist interior of her tender
mouth in a rawly sexual imitation of a far more basic
possession. She moaned as he tugged her thighs apart
and settled his lean hips in the cradle of her pelvis.

He tore his mouth away and thrust her T-shirt out of his way. The worn scrap of lace that cupped her straining breasts was parted with the same summary efficiency and then he bent his dark head and hungrily closed his lips over a pouting roseate nipple. A choked sound broke in her throat. Her spine arched as he flicked his tongue expertly over the sensitive nub and employed his hand on its neglected twin. An explosion of sensation made her jerk and writhe beneath him.

He groaned something and deftly shifted her on to her side. He found her breasts again but this time he inflamed her with maddening little bites that drove her to fever pitch. His hand slid down over her quivering stomach and beneath her leggings to the tangle of curls at the apex of her thighs. The clothing hampering his explorations was wrenched out of the way. Long fingers smoothly sought and found the moist welcome at the very heart of her, and without warning she was suddenly flat on her back again.

Every inch of her body was hot, hungry, aching. She was trembling, shaking, lost to everything but the intense need he had awakened. He drew back from her, hauled his sweater off, and cast it roughly aside, his hands dropping to the waistband of his tight riding breeches as he knelt between her spread thighs. For a split-second he paused, staring down at her with glittering jewelled eyes that blazed with ruthless determination and a desire so powerful that it vibrated from him in sexual waves.

'Bloody hell, I've never felt like this before,' he admitted rawly. 'Nobody's ever made me feel like this before! Getting laid has never been this exciting for me... I feel as if I'm about to ride for the Gold Cup.'

Chrissy had already been unconsciously tugging her T-shirt back down over her exposed body. She hadn't been thinking. Quite frankly, she was far beyond the ability to think. She was not rational. She was possessed by the overwhelming hunger he had unleashed, ready to drag him back to her, as unashamedly impatient as he was. And then she heard the scream, thin and distant and scared, and she reacted instantly, as if someone had jerked a maternal tripwire inside her.

'Rosie!' she gasped, practically falling off the sofa in her haste to reach the source of that frightening cry.

She took the stairs two at a time. Rosie was sitting up rigid in her bed, sobbing. Chrissy wrapped her arms round her. 'It's all right, baby...it's all right,' she soothed with the calm of long practice. 'It was only a silly dream.'

As soon as Rosie felt her touch, heard her voice, the rigidity went out of her small body. She allowed herself to be lowered back on to the pillow. Chrissy smoothed her hair back from her damp brow and, within seconds, Rosie gave a sleepy half-smile, turned on her side, and went back to sleep. If you got there on time, it was always that easy with Rosie.

Still on automatic pilot, Chrissy was backing out of the room when a pair of determined arms imprisoned her from behind.

'I don't think even the fire service moves that fast.' Blaze spun her round and lifted her with equal speed. Closing two lean hands round her thighs, he anchored them smoothly round his lean hips and, without even pausing for breath, he drove her soft lips apart with the force of his mouth in a long, drugging, earth-moving kiss.

The world spun violently around her. She dug her fingers into the luxuriant depths of his black hair, drunk on the sheer intensity of pleasure for several dizzy minutes. He groaned as he bruised his shoulder against an inconveniently situated door-jamb and then lowered her to the bed. That was his mistake. Her lashes lifted and she focused on the elaborate canopy of faded crewel work far above her and the sight twined instantly with a memory from the past.

'Oh, no...' Chrissy whispered in horror, and started to try and sit up.

Blaze, wholly engaged in the intricacies of arranging her to his exact satisfaction, flattened her again with an arrogant hand.

She jack-knifed up on to her knees, both hands holding her oversized T-shirt down in a sudden attack of stricken modesty. 'No!'

'No?' Blaze almost whispered. His voice wasn't quite steady.

Chrissy scrambled frantically off the far side of the bed. 'I'm sorry, but we can't——'

'We most definitely can.' In one long stride, Blaze reached her again.

'I'm s-sorry!' she gasped. 'I didn't m-mean this to go so far——'

'I haven't even crossed the starting line yet. What the hell is going on?' Blaze demanded ferociously. 'Is this some sort of game you play in the hope of getting raped?'

'That's a f-f-f-f-f——' Abruptly, she dived past him, taking him by surprise and fled downstairs.

He found her in the dimly lit sitting-room, curled up in a tight ball in an armchair. He stilled several feet away. Her strained eyes, full of guilt and confusion, skittered over him. He was so incredibly good-looking that she couldn't take her eyes off him even though she knew that he was in a white rage of disbelief.

'I'm s-s-s-sorry,' she stammered painfully.

'I want to know why. Is this pay-back time for three years ago?'

'No!'

'Did I hurt you then?' Brilliant blue eyes probed her shuttered face. 'Is that what this is about? Are you scared?'

'No!' To seize on such an explanation after all the lies she had already told seemed quite inexcusable to her. Soon he would be thinking that he had virtually raped her that night. And the truth was that he had only kissed her, spoken harsh words. A hysterical giggle clogged her throat. She was sinking deeper and deeper into a

quagmire of her own making. The lie and the truth were
becoming blurred as she found herself forced to live the
lie.

'Has there been anyone else since then?' Blaze
prompted with horrific persistence.

More embarrassed than ever, she shook her head. The
speed with which he had controlled his anger startled
her. He could have said a lot of very nasty things to her
and they would have been true. She should have called
a halt far sooner, but she didn't have that capability to
draw on at will. His power over her was the greater. And
either she was a natural born wanton or the unstable
emotions sloshing about inside her were a symptom of
an involvement on her part that ran far deeper than
simple sexual need.

She shivered fearfully.

'Stop that... I am not about to jump your bones
without permission in triplicate. Relax,' Blaze breathed
with a savage edge to his usually cool drawl. 'Are you
afraid of becoming pregnant again? It may be hard for
you to believe, but I wouldn't have risked that.'

'I'm sorry,' she said again. All she wanted to do was
get away from him to probe the depths of her own
confusion.

'If you say that again, I'll——' His exclamation broke
off. Swinging away, she heard him breathe in deeply.
'You really know how to pile on the agony, don't you?
No, that wasn't an accusation, but have you any idea
how I feel? I never get into complicated relationships... you could say I avoid them like the plague. I
know my own limitations better than anyone. I like
women for two things: company and sex. Emotions and
sensitivity don't come into it. There are no strings.'

'You u-use women!' Her voice had a tiny betraying
catch.

'That's another thing about you...' Blaze gritted. 'You
make me so bloody angry! Using is a two-way street,
sweetheart. My first sexual experience was with an as-

sistant matron at school. I was thirteen! Who used whom? When some devious bitch tells the tabloids exactly what I did to her in bed, who used whom? And when I pick up all the bills for the duration of the affair, who is using whom?'

In stark distress, she stared at him. 'I don't want to h-hear any more. I'm not trying to use you!'

'I know... but you are making me feel things I don't want to feel.'

'Let us go, then,' she whispered. 'Why d-did you drag me back tonight?'

'You really don't understand, do you?' He expelled his breath in a hiss. 'I want Rosie.'

Chrissy went rigid. 'I want Rosie'! Short and succinct, no beating about the bush. No pretence that the woman he believed to be Rosie's mother was one tenth as important as the child. The admission burned into her like the careless slash of a knife, and it hurt, oh, lord, it hurt. He had had a natural affinity with Rosie from the very first moment they met. How much was that influencing his willingness to believe that Rosie was his? But she couldn't concentrate on that question. The pain absorbed her and she traced it this time to source. She was falling in love with him. Crazy... insane... suicidal. Falling in love with Blaze couldn't be anything else. She couldn't credit that she had so blithely denied how he was affecting her.

'You want Rosie...' She struggled desperately to focus on the conversation.

A broad shoulder shifted in a slight shrug. 'I really want her... I haven't the slightest desire to duck the responsibility.'

'You didn't want her this afternoon when your l-lawyer came to the rescue!' Chrissy condemned. 'You pushed her away——'

'I had to come to terms with my own shock before I could handle being close to her. I didn't want to see her until I had.' He held her gaze levelly. 'Do you want a drink?'

'No.' She needed her wits about her... that was, what wits she had left.

She watched him splashing whisky into a crystal tumbler. He was barefoot, clad only in the skin-tight riding breeches and a checked shirt he had pulled on and not bothered to button. He was, without doubt, the most gorgeous male she had ever seen. Was that what it was? Some kind of ghastly juvenile infatuation with his looks? But if that was true, why did the rest of him fascinate her so much? She wanted to get inside his head and know exactly what he was thinking, and she knew that never, ever would she have that power.

You got glimpses, hints, occasionally careless confessions, but most of the latter were triggered by sexual arousal. The rest of the time, everything was hidden. She was shut out, distanced, foiled by a self-discipline undoubtedly learnt in childhood. He shared only what he chose to share, and she hated the superficial front he could assume at will. But that front, she registered, was nowhere in evidence now. Not when Rosie was in question.

He was acting entirely out of character. He should have run a mile from the threat of fatherhood! But then possibly the prospect of a child outside the imprisoning bonds of marriage did have appeal for him, she thought uncertainly. 'I want Rosie', she repeated to herself again, angry that she still couldn't concentrate on what was most important. What on earth did he mean when he said that he wanted her sister? Did he mean that he was ready to take charge and Chrissy was free to go?

'I called on Guy for two reasons,' Blaze stated. 'One, he's a close friend. Two, your attitude convinced me that I had to know what rights I had——'

'Rights?'

'Where Rosie's concerned. You could say that Guy helped to clarify how very few rights unmarried fathers have. I can demand visitation rights, but you could probably block me on that if you could convince a court that seeing me is upsetting her——'

Her brows pleated anxiously. 'But——'

'Hear me out,' he told her flatly. 'I haven't supported you since she was born, so that doesn't make me look too good. You've been having a very hard time surviving and I've been living a highly visible and far from respectable existence, broadly based on the old wine, women and song adage. I haven't lived like responsible father material. Short of bribing people to lie about your fitness as a mother in court, I really have no chance of winning custody——'

'C-custody? Why would you want custody?' she broke in shakily, beginning to drown afresh in the horror of the way in which a lie could grow and grow like a monster until it overshadowed her whole existence. Of course, she had nothing to fear. As soon as Elaine came to her senses, which she hoped she was already well on the road to doing, she could confess the lie.

He sank down with innate grace into the armchair opposite her. 'You could meet another man, get married, and sooner or later I'd be pushed out of her life. Guy tells me it happens all the time. People start out with good intentions and promises, and then other relationships get in the way. Divorced fathers regularly lose out on contact with their children. I'm not prepared to let that happen to me——'

'Blaze...you're taking this all too s-seriously... You only found out today... I mean, don't you think this is all a little premature?'

'I've already lost out on two and a half years of her life,' he reminded her with fierce emphasis. 'I intend to be there for her from now on. She's not going to grow up the way I did!'

She waited, squirming with guilt.

He sprang upright, studied her fulminatingly. 'When my father found out about me, he wanted to have contact with me, but my mother wouldn't allow it. That was *her* revenge. When she died, he came to see me at school without my grandfather's permission. I didn't want to know him! This was the guy I blamed for screwing up my mother's life... mine too, for that matter,' he admitted harshly. 'I knew he was married. I knew he had a baby son. And I hated him for that. I wouldn't have anything to do with him. He felt really guilty about me and he had persuaded his wife that it was their duty to offer me a home with them in Spain.'

He threw back a gulp of whisky and vented a rueful laugh. 'He was... what was that expression you used?... "intellectually challenged"? A handsome playboy, constitutionally incapable of fidelity, but basically an OK guy. His wife sat quietly in the corner and you could see that she was sick to the stomach at the threat of having to house her husband's bastard! Jaime couldn't see that, though. He really thought that with Barb out of the picture I could be part of their family. He had touching faith in what he called our "bond of blood". And I told the poor bastard to go to hell...'

Chrissy ached for him. Her wide eyes dampened.

'He was persistent, though. He wrote... I trashed the letters without reading them. Eventually they stopped coming. The irony of it is...' He laughed with wry amusement. 'The real irony is that if he had approached my grandfather first I would have been parcelled off to Spain on the next flight!'

'You mean... you mean your grandfather wouldn't have wanted to keep you?' she pressed in a tone of distress.

Blaze drained his glass, set it down. 'I only wanted to illustrate my point. I bitterly regretted never knowing my father. I was too proud to approach him when I was an adult myself. I'm not saying I missed out on anything that special. I don't think we would have been soul mates, but maybe we could at least have been friends.' His sensual mouth tautened. 'It was a hell of a shock when Jaime and his family went down in that plane crash...'

'It must have been,' she whispered sickly.

'It was too late then to wish I'd spent some time with him,' he breathed harshly. 'Too late then to get to know the half-brother and -sister I'd never met. Most times in life, you don't get second chances... I certainly didn't. I can't even begin to describe how I felt when I inherited Jaime's money...'

Although it was hard for her to understand fully what he had been through, she felt raw with sympathy, and she bowed her head to hide her feelings.

'He never forgot that I was his first-born son. Even if my half-brother and -sister had survived, I would have inherited more than they did,' he revealed tautly. 'He was a multimillionaire and I got the whole lot. I didn't want it... This was the guy I rejected while he was still alive... It seemed all wrong that I should profit from his death...'

'But if he wanted you to have it...'

'In the end I came to that conclusion too, but even though I endow all his favourite charities I still feel bloody guilty. That's why I want to be there for Rosie now,' he said again. 'I want her to have it all. And she needs security.'

'I agree,' she forced herself to say. 'But——'

'No buts,' he incised softly. 'I never wanted children of my own. I never wanted to do to any child what my parents did to me. I didn't want the responsibility. It was a purely self-centred decision. I have always taken great care never to run the smallest risk of getting any woman pregnant... only now I find out that just once I didn't take care and the whole picture changes out of all recognition!'

Should she tell him the truth now? Should she tell him that she had lied? What would happen when he stopped concentrating on Rosie? Sixth sense warned her that he would turn with renewed intensity to his desire for re-

venge on Elaine. And if Chrissy told him that her sister
was pregnant and that that was why she had told the lie
in the first instance, he would never believe her. He would
think it was just another lie, because Elaine would not
admit that she was carrying Steve's baby. Dully, she
realised that she was caught between a rock and a hard
place. She would be damned if she did speak up and
equally damned if she didn't! Until she could confirm
that Elaine had gone back to Steve, her sister's unborn
child could only be protected by her lie and her silence.

'You are so quiet,' he censured. 'Anyone might be
forgiven for thinking that none of this had anything to
do with you.'

Events had already moved far beyond her control. She
was a woman on a cliff-edge waiting for a final push.
'I don't know what to say to you,' she admitted shakily,
and it was the most truth she had spoken that day.

'Rosie is happy here but you can't stay on as my
housekeeper now...'

Her stomach lurched sickly. Now she saw where the
big, impressive build-up had been leading. He was about
to suggest they move out! The selfish toad! He wanted
Rosie, but presumably at a discreet distance and in small,
bearable doses.

A line of dark colour demarcated his hard cheekbones. 'The gutter Press never leave me alone. That's
never bothered me before but I really don't want you
and Rosie to be trailed out into the public eye by the
tabloids. I've never given a damn about what's written
about me but I don't want you torn apart——'

'You d-didn't give a damn about that yesterday!' she
muttered tightly.

'But you have centred my priorities wonderfully since
yesterday,' he drawled with sardonic bite. 'Yesterday was
a century ago.'

She wished he would get to the point. She was sitting
on the edge of her seat, her nails grooving crescents into
her clenched palms as she waited. She wanted her every

low expectation of Blaze Kenyon confirmed. He wanted them out from under this roof and fast before they could cause him any further embarrassment.

'The truth is...' he hesitated, his sensual mouth tightening into an unrelentingly grim line '...and I never thought I would ever hear myself say this...but needs must when the devil rides—and bloody hell, he's been busy in my corner of Berkshire!' he muttered savagely half under his breath. 'We have to get married, fast.'

CHAPTER EIGHT

CHRISSY was welded to her chair. She was transfixed like a graven image, shocked green eyes glued to him. She didn't believe he had actually said that. He couldn't have actually said that, could he?

'We would live exactly as we do now...more or less,' Blaze went on after a reflective pause. 'You get a home, all the money you can spend, and security, and I get you and Rosie. What you might term a mutually beneficial exchange of needs.'

Her tongue crept out to moisten her bone-dry lips. She swallowed hard. 'You're not s-serious?'

'If I weren't, I'd be a damned fool to suggest it!' he pointed out scathingly.

'But you can't have thought this through,' she protested weakly.

'I know exactly what I want to do,' he rebutted. 'I don't want to figure in Rosie's life as an occasional father, nor do I want a parade of "uncles" through her life...'

As Chrissy grasped his meaning, she coloured and lifted her chin. 'There isn't going to be any such parade!'

Blaze dealt her an impatient glance. 'At least be realistic, Chrissy. You're unlikely to remain celibate until she's eighteen!'

'People don't just leap into marriage these days for a child's b-benefit,' she dared.

'I do and you will,' Blaze delivered. 'To be blunt, I don't see what the problem is. Sexually, we're very compatible. Marriages are built on far less. Rosie deserves the security of two parents and a proper home.'

'Yes, but it's not that simple——'

'It's exactly that simple. I want Rosie to have everything I didn't have.'

And that was his real motivation, Chrissy registered ruefully. He had been born outside marriage and, by the fleeting references he made to the mother he had evidently called Barb, there had been no stability in his childhood. Suddenly, she felt remarkably foolish. Why was she sitting here anxiously arguing with him on the question of a marriage that would never take place? She was turning into a candidate for the funny farm! Within a few days at most, she would be in a position to tell him the truth. In the light of the plans he was already making for her sister's future in the belief that Rosie was his, the truth might well hit him even harder than the original lie.

He was reacting so positively to the idea that he was a father. She could never have dreamt that his first and most overriding concern would be for Rosie's welfare... but it was. Dear heaven, he was actually prepared to marry to provide Rosie with the kind of security he had never had himself! How could she ever have foreseen that? This was the male who barely two weeks ago had said of himself that he would never get married. 'No reason to, every reason not to.' But evidently he found Rosie sufficient reason.

'Well?' Blaze prompted impatiently.

Dear lord, he wanted an answer. A band of tension throbbed like a ring of steel round her brow. She was exhausted and in turmoil. Tonight she had so nearly ended up in his bed. She turned her troubled gaze wretchedly from him. She wanted him, and in the back of her mind lurked all the fantasies that had probably encouraged many other women in his past to hope...that somehow *she* would be different from all the others before her, that somehow *she* would be the one he would decide to stay with, the one he would love.

Although she shrank from the dreadful scene ahead when she told him the truth, and the inevitable conclusion, which would be their departure, it would be the wisest finale in the circumstances. Otherwise, sooner or later she would end up in his bed, and a transitory affair would do nothing for her self-respect. He was a very male animal and he wanted to have sex with her...that was all. At no stage had he even pretended that she touched him any more deeply. Even if it hadn't been for the lie, there was no future here for her.

'Have y-you ever been in love?' she heard herself ask, the impulsive question simply leaping off her tongue.

'No.' He didn't even have to consider his answer. 'Are you planning to give me an answer?'

She refused to meet his glittering gaze. 'I'll think about it.'

'Playing hard to get, Chrissy?' he drawled mockingly.

He expected a positive answer, no doubt about that. A lack of self-confidence was not one of his failings. He had condescended to offer marriage. He had anticipated an eager acceptance. And why should she weary herself arguing with him about something that was never going to happen? It would take at least a couple of weeks to arrange a marriage. And this farce would be over far sooner.

He hunkered down athletically in front of her. Lean fingers pushed up her chin almost playfully. 'You said that if you thought I was all there was in your future you'd kill yourself! But that was because I let you down three years ago...'

'Was it?' She couldn't resist fighting him.

Sapphire eyes tracked over her triangular face intently. 'I didn't see you in my future either, but right now I can't imagine it without you. I guess I've got used to having you around. I feel comfortable with you...' Her small teeth visibly clenched. Comfortable...like an old chair or a slipper. 'When I'm not feeling sexually frustrated,' he finished with a certain predatory huskiness.

'I can always tell when you're thinking about s-sex!'

'I hope so... Recently, it's been twenty-four hours a day...and I would hate to think this misery was one-sided!' He tugged one of her hands free and pressed his mouth hungrily to the fleshy mount below her thumb, letting her feel the graze of his teeth, and she trembled, feeling as if her bones were melting beneath her over-sensitive skin. 'If I hurt you the last time, I'm sorry... I can promise you that it won't be like that again.'

Her cheeks reddening, she dragged her hand from his, but it took every ounce of will-power she possessed to execute that feat of self-denial. When he looked at her like that, she felt hypnotised, weak, utterly helpless. 'Blaze, I——'

'You're going to marry me,' he told her. 'It's what I want.'

'And do you generally get what you want?'

He sent her a mocking smile and vaulted upright. 'Always.'

'I think it's time I went to b-bed,' she muttered, rising unsteadily from the chair, but she didn't want to go; she didn't want to leave him. She was painfully aware that in a very short space of time Blaze would hate her for the lies she had told him, and this time there would be no offer of a free pardon to bolster her fall.

'I've got a couple of calls to make.'

She didn't sleep very well, tired though she was. She dreamt that she was getting married to Blaze and in the middle of the ceremony Elaine came in and interrupted the proceedings just like the bad fairy in the story of the Sleeping Beauty. Only instead of delivering a mere curse in punishment, Elaine walked off with the bridegroom and Chrissy was left standing at the altar alone in front of a congregation roaring with laughter. She woke up, tear-stained and trembling. It had been unbelievably real.

There was a note on the kitchen table when she came downstairs.

'Gone to see Theo', it said. There was no signature, but she held it for a second or two and her eyes prickled stupidly. Blaze never made the tiniest attempt to explain absences. Unless you caught him on the way out of the door, he simply vanished. That he had taken the time to scrawl even four words of explanation underlined the alteration he now saw in their relationship. But it was all a lie, *all* a lie, she reminded herself painfully. Of course, it would never occur to him that she hadn't a clue who Theo was. Writing a note had been enough of a challenge.

The builders were now at the stage of converting part of the attics into a self-contained flat. For a house-keeper, Chrissy guessed, and that was where she would have been moving with Rosie, had they been staying. A washing machine, a tumble-drier and a state-of-the-art vacuum cleaner were delivered mid-morning. She stood there staring at them incredulously while they were off-loaded into the rear hall. Blaze must actually have gone to the trouble of buying them. When? Yesterday? Today?

In something of a daze, she went to answer the door when the bell rang. It was Elaine, rather ostentatiously sheathed in a stunning pure white suit that flattered every perfect curve. 'It's a wonder you can look me in the face!' she said witheringly. 'I made an absolute ass of myself with Blaze yesterday, thanks to you! Where is he? I want to see him.'

Chrissy tensed in alarm. It seemed she had not been so convincing where her sister was concerned. 'He's out.'

Elaine's lips tightened. 'Why did you lie like that? It wasn't until I went home again that it occurred to me that Blaze was as shocked as I was! He flatly denied being the father of your child... said he had never had anything to do with you! He asked me if I had been drinking!'

Chrissy took her into the drawing-room. Rosie was painting in the kitchen. She would be all right on her own for a few minutes.

'I can't believe that *I* believed you!' Elaine vented angrily.

Chrissy was thinking fast. 'I had no idea you were planning to confront him. You see, he remembers nothing about that night and he certainly knew nothing about Rosie until you chose to tell him!'

That angle hadn't occurred to Elaine.

Chrissy pressed on, 'I'd never have had the nerve to tell him about Rosie...so really I should be thanking you——'

'Thanking me?' Elaine slung at her. 'Thanking me for what?'

'For doing us a very big favour.' Chrissy smiled widely at her infuriated sister. 'You see, unlike you, Blaze does believe that Rosie is his child, and not only is he willing to accept that fact, he also wants Rosie... He's willing to acknowledge her...'

'You're lying again. Blaze doesn't even like kids!' Elaine asserted.

'*Well*,' Chrissy murmured with another smile, 'he certainly likes Rosie. In fact, he's asked me to marry him——'

'I'd have to be brain-dead to swallow that!' Elaine sneered. 'Blaze Kenyon has to be about the last male alive likely to start talking marriage because he finds out some sordid one-night stand resulted in an unwanted baby!'

'Perhaps you're forgetting *his* background,' Chrissy suggested smoothly. 'He grew up as an illegitimate child without a father. He's absolutely determined that Rosie won't!'

'Even if the kid was his, he wouldn't marry you.' Elaine swore harshly, her beautiful face fierce with certainty.

'Elaine, why don't you go home to Steve? Why don't you put this behind you?' Chrissy suddenly pleaded.

'Leaving you a clear field? You've got to be joking!' Elaine spat. 'And I still refuse to believe that kid is his! Show me the birth certificate...show me some real proof! You were totally fat and unattractive three years ago. I don't believe he would have looked at you, even drunk! So if that brat isn't his, who did father her?'

Chrissy stood stock-still. Elaine read the flash of dismay that briefly froze her kid sister's features. 'She is Blaze's child,' Chrissy insisted tremulously.

'Is she...? I wonder,' Elaine breathed absently. 'You were the most frightful po-faced little prude at seventeen. When I think about it, I find it very hard to credit that you just fell into bed with Blaze of all people.'

Without warning, Elaine spun and walked back out to the hall, seemingly eager to be gone.

'Kissy...see my picher!' Rosie came running out of the kitchen waving her painting.

Elaine paused with her hand resting on the front door. Her keen eyes narrowed as they rested on Rosie's animated little face. A soft intake of breath escaped her and then suddenly, disturbingly, she smiled back at Chrissy. 'I'll be seeing you...some time soon, I expect.'

Rigid with tension, Chrissy watched her climb into the Porsche. Could Elaine suspect the truth? That Rosie was their mother's child? No, how could she? Elaine didn't have an atom of evidence on which to base such an assumption. It wouldn't even cross her mind that Belle could have given birth to another baby shortly before she died. Why should it?

It was after five when Blaze returned. Sheathed in a superbly tailored grey suit, he stood in the kitchen doorway watching her for several seconds before he spoke, an odd smile playing about his wide mouth. Then Rosie hit his knees and he scooped her up and scrutinised her with unashamed intensity. 'Do you think she looks like me?' he asked lazily. 'I don't see any obvious Kenyon features. She is dark, but her hair isn't as black as mine and she has your pale complexion.'

Chrissy bit painfully at her lower lip and simply ducked the issue. She cleared her throat. 'Elaine came here today...'

'Really...? I hope she doesn't plan to become a regular visitor.'

'I th-think you should tell her that w-whatever you
had with her is over...'

'I didn't have anything with her,' Blaze dismissed.

'You should tell *her* th-that,' Chrissy persisted tightly.
Blaze, she had decided, was the only person capable of
convincing Elaine that she was wasting her time.

'Chrissy, as far as I'm concerned, Elaine doesn't exist.'
His intonation was one of cool finality, but Chrissy ignored the warning.

'Elaine n-needs to know that now,' she repeated
doggedly.

'She'll know when we're married.'

But by then it might be too late, Chrissy wanted to
scream in frustration. As yet, Elaine was unconvinced
that Blaze was out of reach. She was still perfectly
fectly capable of going ahead with the abortion. 'But
that——'

Dense black lashes dropped low over narrowed
sapphire eyes. 'Do I need to rent a billboard to get the
message across?' he drawled with icy bite. 'You deal with
your bitch of a sister on your own. Frankly, I prefer not
to be reminded of your family connections.'

Cut to the bone, Chrissy flushed and studied the table.
She felt about an inch tall. Lifting the post lying on the
table, Blaze strode out. Slowly but surely, however, a
sense of angry injustice filled her. How dared he
condemn her family connections when only those connections had prompted him to give her this job? Deliberately playing on her ignorance, he had brought them
up here for a purpose. That purpose had been to use
both her and Rosie as a weapon against her father!

Was Blaze even now playing a game of deception with
her? He had flatly refused to tell Elaine that he was finished with her. Could that be because he was secretly
determined to continue stringing her sister along? How
far had that desire for revenge already taken Blaze? He
had convinced Elaine that he wanted her. How much

time had they spent together in London? Had he made love to her sister... had they shared a bed?

Bile burned Chrissy's throat. She felt physically sick at the stark imagery flooding her mind. Her sister and Blaze, hotly entwined on tangled sheets. He despised Elaine, but that did not mean that he would not have touched her, did it? Blaze was a very male animal and Elaine was very beautiful. Sex without emotion. He was capable of that... oh, yes, Chrissy was painfully aware that Blaze was capable of such an act. Indeed she suspected that sex *with* emotion might present him with a tougher challenge.

He glanced up from the letter in his hand when he saw her in the doorway. 'I have a secretary starting next week. We'll work in here until the builders complete the office in the old stable block.'

Chrissy bit down on the soft underside of her lower lip. The tiny pain spurred her on. 'What did you have planned f-for Elaine?'

His striking bone-structure clenched. 'I really don't think you want to know. You're the compassionate, forgiving type... I'm not,' he admitted with chilling emphasis. 'I wanted to hurt Elaine and I had every intention of doing it. I would have enjoyed it as well. I would have broken her with pleasure...'

Pale and shocked, Chrissy stared back at him.

'You are all that stands between Elaine and retribution. She ought to be kissing your feet in gratitude. You and Rosie are her only protection,' he drawled very softly. 'Marrying you will prohibit retaliation on my part... Does that ease your sisterly anxieties?'

No, it terrified her! If she disappeared, Elaine would go ahead with the termination. If she told Blaze the truth, he would return with renewed savagery to his campaign of revenge. Only if she actually went through with marrying him would Elaine give up and go home... but she couldn't possibly go to those lengths... could she?

'As for your father,' he continued drily, 'I have no further interest there either. Hamilton Enterprises is on the brink of bankruptcy.'

Chrissy was shattered by the cold indifference which distinguished that revelation. 'Bankrupt? He was doing so w-well...I thought...' Her voice tailed away.

'He should never have sold the fast-food chain. He knew that business from the ground up. He made some very unwise investments with the proceeds. I doubt if he'll be in the neighbourhood for much longer.'

Chrissy had no great affection for her father but she was distressed on his behalf. He had made money his god, his whole reason for existence. Shorn of his wealth, what would he do?

'You're actually feeling sorry for the bastard!' Blaze raked at her, tight-mouthed, taking her by surprise.

'He is my f-father.'

'"A poor thing but mine own". Remember that when you promise to love, honour and obey I expect one hundred per cent loyalty as well.' Brilliant sapphire-blue eyes bored into her in unashamed intimidation. 'And I wouldn't like to be in your shoes if I don't get it...'

Her strained gaze dropped first. She was in turmoil.

'Chrissy, nobody gets to select their relations,' he murmured. 'You have nothing in common with Elaine but a surname. You don't lie and cheat and manipulate and bitch. Don't make your family a bone of contention between us.'

Of the four sins mentioned, she stood guilty of every one. She couldn't meet his eyes. She had put herself in this strait-jacket. But Blaze had forced her into it, she told herself, desperate to share out some of the blame. Elaine's unborn child was the only truly innocent party. If only she could have trusted Blaze enough to tell him the truth. But Blaze was seethingly bitter and so chillingly desirous of revenge that she did not dare risk the likely outcome.

'Come here.' A cool hand curved to her stiff spine and pressed her out to the hall. A gold-coloured box with an impressive logo, accompanied by several bags, lay in a careless heap just inside the front door. 'We're going out tonight. Dining with the Allans. I bought you something to wear.'

'Going out?' she whispered, still dazed by what had passed between them.

'I want you dressed to impress.' He piled the box and the bags into her nerveless grasp. 'Floss is coming over to make dinner for Rosie and babysit...so you can pamper yourself for a couple of hours.'

'The Allans?' She was totally taken aback at the idea of dining out with him.

'He's an owner. I train five of his horses.'

He had bought her clothes. Contrarily, she wanted nothing to fit, didn't want to be reminded of the kind of womanising expertise which was underwritten in such a confident gesture. And, worse, the lie was beginning to go public. Appearing with her at a dinner party was a sort of statement. Once again the lie was growing in stature. But right now there was nothing she could do about that, she told herself squarely. She had to sit Elaine out and call her bluff for the baby's sake.

After a long, lazy bath, she opened the box and drew out a deceptively simple black shift dress with a half-sleeve and a low back. It was a size eight, spot-on. The bags variously produced high-heeled black patent shoes adorned with suede and *diamanté* inserts matched to an evening purse, gossamer-fine, nearly black stockings and an accompanying lingerie set in silk and lace that brought hot colour to her cheeks. And every single item fitted like a glove.

Blaze was in the drawing-room, lost in the depths of some racing publication. She cleared her throat nervously. He threw down the magazine, sprang up, and treated her to an arrested glance. Sapphire eyes flamed over the tumble of mahogany curls framing her flushed triangular face, lingered on the ripe red of her mouth and went on to trace the sleek fit of the dress hugging her slender curves and accentuating the long, elegant length of her legs.

'Who's Demi Moore?' he breathed softly. 'You look stunning.'

Chrissy shuffled off one foot on to the other, wreathed in self-consciousness, certain he could only be saying that to bolster her confidence. In her opinion, Blaze was the one who looked stunning. In a dinner-jacket, he took her breath away.

'I have only one complaint,' he murmured. 'Black was supposed to make you look older. It doesn't. You look sixteen, all sweet and pink and breathless, as if you're about to go out on your first date...'

Getting even pinker, she averted her eyes. It was. Her first real date. There had been no boyfriends before she left home. As Elaine had delighted in reminding her, she had been totally unattractive. And she had only had a couple of months at college before her mother's problems had taken all her freedom away. Apart from a few group outings, she was just about as hatefully inexperienced as she looked.

'I want you to wear this...' He flipped open a jewellery case lying on the marble mantelpiece and extracted a slender diamond necklace that glittered exquisitely in the firelight. 'It was Barb's...'

'I can't!' Chrissy gasped, awash with guilt. Ignoring the assurance, he flipped her round and deftly clasped the necklace round her throat. Her fingers pressed it shakily. 'But it was your mother's...'

'It's getting late.' He gave her a gentle push towards the door.

Floss came out to the hall, clutching Rosie's hand and smiling broadly. 'I am so happy for you both...'

'Never thought you'd see the day, did you?' Blaze quipped.

'Why did you t-tell Floss about us?' Chrissy demanded in the Ferrari.

'Hamish has been treating me like a child molester since he overheard Elaine yesterday,' Blaze imparted drily.

'W-what?'

'You were a teenager and I was ten years older. A sparkling self-defence eludes me.'

Chrissy squirmed in the passenger seat, increasingly unnerved by the way the lie was spreading like an insidious poison to draw in new victims.

The Allans lived in what had probably once been a plain country farmhouse. Now it was a mansion-farmhouse, awash with chintz and extensions. Davis Allan, a spare man in his early sixties, greeted them at the door. 'You're always the last to arrive, Blaze... Ah, who's this?'

Dear God, she wanted to sink. She was here without invitation!

Davis peered short-sightedly at her. 'You're not Lesley, are you?'

'Chrissy,' Blaze delivered calmly.

'I can't keep up with your harem, old chap.' Davis slapped his shoulder and had a hearty laugh. Chrissy's cheeks burned. She wanted to chain Blaze to a wall and slowly kill him.

The second she met Janine Allan's eyes, she knew she was an unwelcome surprise. Davis's wife was about twenty years younger, a painfully thin blonde whose entire concentration focused with embarrassing fervour on Blaze, to the exclusion of her other half-dozen guests. What Blaze wanted to drink, where he should sit, what he had been doing dominated the whole conversation until they moved to the dining-room.

'You sh-shouldn't have brought me when I wasn't invited,' Chrissy hissed on the way through.

'All my invitations include..."and partner".'

'You're very young to be a housekeeper,' Janine remarked with saccharine sweetness. Somebody audibly choked back laughter.

'I like housekeepers young and fresh,' Blaze drawled smoothly.

Chrissy's teeth clenched.

'I've been hearing the most astounding stories about you,' Janine confided to the table at large.

Her husband coughed. 'I don't think——'

'That Chrissy isn't really my housekeeper?' Blaze mocked. 'That one was *true*.'

Again somebody laughed. Janine appeared anything but happy to have her suspicions confirmed.

Blaze rested a lean hand on Chrissy's and lounged lazily back in his chair. 'You see, Chrissy and I are getting married——'

'Married?' her hostess ejaculated incredulously. Her husband spilt his wine. Nobody laughed; everyone stared. Chrissy turned very pale, appalled at the convincing ease with which he had made that announcement.

Davis proposed a toast. There was much jocularity about the confinements of matrimony. Perking up, Janine began to survey Chrissy with pity, rather than envy.

'Aren't you brave to take him on?' she gasped in a meant-to-be-heard undertone as they left at the end of the longest and most hideous evening Chrissy had ever had to endure. 'Still, I suppose marriage is the *one* thing he hasn't tried!'

'That's what having an affair with your secretary did for Davis,' Blaze told Chrissy a few minutes later, sending the Ferrari raking too fast down the paved driveway. 'A lesson to us all! His first wife was a darling. I can't stand bitchy women! If she does that again, Davis will have to take his horses elsewhere. They're not worth a damn anyway.'

Without warning, he stopped the car, released his seatbelt and reached for her. It all seemed to happen in one movement. Passing one practised arm round her slight shoulders, he leant over her and took her unprepared mouth in a savagely demanding assault that rocked her from her head to her toes. It was explosive.

Sure fingers rested on a slender thigh, flirted teasingly with the silky skin above the stocking-top. 'I needed that,' he groaned against her mouth.

A car horn shrilled in three staccato bursts as it passed them.

Blaze laughed huskily. 'Bang goes my image. That was a couple of our fellow guests. I'm off to London first thing tomorrow. I spend half my life on the road...'

It took immense self-discipline but she was making a recovery. By dint of blocking out awareness of those playful fingers on her thigh, the other set of fingers stroking the nape of her neck, she contrived it for several driven seconds. 'W-why did you tell them that we were getting married?'

'Since we'll be married the day after tomorrow, it didn't seem too premature.'

Chrissy froze. 'The d-day after tomorrow? You're out of your m-mind... You're joking!'

'Why do you think I went to see Theo?'

'I don't even kn-know who Theo is!' she snapped.

He frowned in surprise. 'He's my godfather. Who else would I approach when I need a special licence?'

'A s-special licence?'

Blaze frowned down at her. 'If we wait, we give the tabloids a field-day! Sooner or later, someone's going to talk to the Press. You and Rosie will be labelled as my secret mistress and child. I don't want that. Even Theo understood that indecent haste was a necessity and, frankly, he was so afraid that I'd never marry, he couldn't shell out the licence fast enough! He probably thinks that if we wait, I'll change my mind. Actually, he's wrong...'

'Th-Theo is a vicar...' she whispered in growing horror.

'A bishop. He's already contacted the local vicar. He wants to officiate at the ceremony, probably in the hope of lending a bit of class to a less than stylish bolt to the church. Do you mind that?'

'M-mind what?' Chrissy mumbled.

He groaned with exasperation. 'How much wine did you drink tonight? Do you mind that it won't be a proper wedding? You can have a dress if you want, blinding white if you like... Nobody cares about only virgins wearing white these days...'

'No,' she conceded in a whisper of sound, her stomach turning over, not once but repeatedly. With difficulty, she swallowed down hysteria. 'I can't m-marry you, Blaze!'

'Of course you can.' He fired the Ferrari as if she hadn't spoken.

'I mean it... I really m-mean it... I can't!' she cried.

'I am not listening to this,' he asserted drily, drawing up in front of the Hall.

'Goodnight,' she said starkly a few minutes later when they were inside and Floss had taken her leave.

'What the hell is the matter with you?' With a powerful hand, he swung her round to face him before she could make it up the stairs to sanctuary.

'N-nothing... I'm just... just not feeling very well.' It was true.

His grip on her arm relaxed. A dark flush underscored his cheekbones. His mouth tightened. 'Couldn't you simply have told me that?'

'I'm just v-very tired... all the excitement, the a-arguments,' she stumbled.

Something flashed in his concerned gaze. He raised an almost awkward hand to her strained face and then dropped it again without touching her. He hovered for a split-second, looking uncharacteristically uncertain of himself, and then stepped back, leaving her free to pass him.

* * *

It was dawn when she finally slept, wakening with a start only when someone gently shook her shoulder. She sat up. 'What on earth...?'

'Blaze even cancelled the builders so that you could sleep in peace,' Floss informed her cheerfully. 'And you must have needed it, to sleep this late...'

It was after three in the afternoon. Startled, Chrissy breathed, 'Blaze?'

'He's gone down to London.'

As soon as she came downstairs, Chrissy headed for the phone. She would tell Elaine that they were getting married tomorrow. Surely even Elaine could not disbelieve that? Surely that would be sufficient to send her home safely to Steve? But nobody answered her call. She paced the floor, wondering if Elaine had already departed, scared to hope, never mind face how the heck she was to get herself out of the predicament she had put herself in.

It was after seven when her repeated phone calls finally received an answer. Her sister's voice, cool and calm, came on the line.

'Blaze and I are getting married t-tomorrow...' Chrissy breathed shakily.

'You may be driving to the church,' Elaine responded with a derisive laugh, 'but I can assure you that you won't be getting married tomorrow or any other day.'

Chrissy swallowed hard. 'How...h-how can you——?'

'You'll find out.'

The dead tone hummed deafeningly loud in Chrissy's ear. Elaine had put the phone down and left it off the hook. Chrissy was still trying to raise an answer when the doorbell went an hour later.

It was Hamish. 'Blaze couldn't get through on the phone. He told me to tell you that he won't be back tonight.' His weathered features were set in familiar lines of grim disapproval. 'Probably off on a bender to steel himself up for the wedding...'

'Thank you, Hamish.' Chrissy was beyond even being insulted. She was ready to tear her hair out in despair.

'He's an absolute disgrace!' Hamish continued fierily. 'Taking advantage of a young girl and only doing the right thing by you at the last ditch! He ought to be ashamed of himself...and he's not—you needn't tell me that; I know. He's in cracking good form!'

Hamish had gone before she managed to hinge her dropped jaw up again. Now she could rejoice in the knowledge that she had Hamish's sympathy, she thought, on the edge of hysteria. But dear heaven, what was she going to do? What had Elaine meant? What was she getting at? Chrissy knew that if she went to the church that was the furthest she could go. She could not go through with the marriage. At the church, she would have to tell the truth. The lie had reached its limits, leaving her in a terrifyingly tight corner.

CHAPTER NINE

'YOU look lovely...' Floss's voice trailed off uneasily. The older woman sensed that something was very wrong, but Chrissy's strained pallor did not invite questions.

A heady combination of fear and desperation had strung Chrissy up so tight that one wrong word would have catapulted her into tears. All she could think about was what lay ahead of her at the church. Foolishly she had not expected Floss to involve herself in the preparations a bride was expected to revel in, any more than she had expected Floss to present her smilingly with the dress that Blaze had sent up from London the day before.

It was the soft pink of candy-floss, only vaguely bridal but decidedly floaty and romantic. Somehow the fact that Blaze had actually chosen the dress underlined the extent of the deception she had practised. He thought this was his wedding-day. He really did believe that. This wasn't some nightmare she was mercifully about to wake up from... No, it was paralysingly real.

Dear God, how would Blaze feel when she exploded the truth on him? Why had she ever let it go this far? At the church, of all places...scarcely the scenario for such a shattering revelation. And his godfather, the bishop, waiting there to perform a ceremony that would not take place! If Blaze had come home last night, she would have told him. Later on, she had phoned Floss and asked if she knew where Blaze was staying, but Floss had had no idea and had instead teased her about bridal nerves.

'Pinch your cheeks,' Hamish urged as she climbed into the car. 'You look like a ghost.'

She wished she were one, dead and safely buried. Until now, she had rigorously suppressed her own feelings for

Blaze. Her own emotions had seemed irrelevant and self-indulgent when set against the far more important issue of protecting Elaine's unborn child. But now, all of a sudden, she was wallowing in those emotions and out of control. She loved him, saw every fault he had but still loved him. She had never really quite believed that love would be like that. But it was. It wasn't blind, it was all-encompassing.

She knew he didn't love her, but she did think he was carelessly fond of her. It wasn't much, but she was about to lose even that. He would despise her. The deception had been unforgivable. He had been very honest with her once the chips were down, but all she had done was lie and lie and lie. And after today she would never see him again...ever. She had packed their cases late last night, ready for the fast departure that would be forced on them.

'I see word's slipped out. Blaze won't like that.'

Surfacing from her self-absorption, Chrissy glanced out of the windscreen as Hamish swung into the grounds of the church. There were people everywhere. Her fearful gaze darted over locals propped up by the railings to the nearest man with a camera rushing in their direction. The Press... She wanted to cringe.

Abruptly the door opened. Blaze, seemingly appearing out of nowhere, reached in to clasp her hand and pull her out at speed. 'Bloody vultures,' he grated furiously, misinterpreting the look of stark panic etched on her pale, tense face.

'Give us a break, Blaze!' one of the journalists groaned as, by dint of forging an aggressive path and keeping her head down, Blaze deprived anyone of the chance of a good picture.

'I have something I have to t-tell y-you,' Chrissy stammered as he trailed her into the dim, shadowy vestibule of the church. 'I——'

Slamming the heavy door, Blaze turned her round and held her at arm's length. Glittering sapphire-blue eyes moved from the top of her head to the soles of her feet and slowly back up again. 'You are *so* pretty in pink,' he murmured in an intense undertone that burnished flags of colour in her pale cheeks.

Thrown off-balance, she was captured by that devouring stare. Briefly she was lost. 'I...I have t-to...I have——'

'Blaze?' Another, cooler voice intervened.

Dropping Chrissy's hands, Blaze swung round. 'What the hell are you doing here?'

Momentarily Elaine froze, her bright, exultant smile sliding away. Her recovery, however, was swift. 'I've been here longer than you have, darling. I've been waiting for the bride's arrival in the clock tower,' she imparted with a little shiver. 'And damned cold and uncomfortable it was too. I do hope you'll appreciate the amount of effort I've been put to in getting hold of this...'

Chrissy was paralysed to the spot. Elaine was holding out a folded document.

Ignoring the offer, Blaze attempted to brush past her sister.

'It's Rosie's birth certificate...I really do think you should take the time to look at it.' Elaine thrust the document into Blaze's hand.

Chrissy's knees threatened to give way. Elaine had got in first, but how...how? How could she possibly have found out when Rosie was born? How could she have even suspected that Rosie was their mother's child?

'The brat is the living spit of Dennis Carruthers!' Elaine dealt Chrissy a contemptuous glance of distaste. 'I had to go down to London for the evidence. I knew the name of the solicitor Belle used for her divorce settlement. She had approached him for advice when Dennis was arrested. I told him that Belle was dead and that I was very anxious to trace my little sister, who was looking after our mother's child. It worked like a dream. He had a copy of the birth certificate in his file. He had it photocopied for me...'

Chrissy wasn't listening to Elaine. She was watching Blaze. Time seemed to slow to a dulled, torturous thud in her eardrums as he impatiently shook open the certificate. She watched as he went white beneath his bronzed skin, the stark beauty of his bone-structure cruelly accentuated as his facial muscles tensed with shock. The hand at her spine stilled and then began to drum a silent tattoo before it abruptly fell away. She watched as his dense lashes dropped low over his piercing gaze, almost brushing his cheekbones as he took a second lightning-fast look at the birth certificate.

Time was speeding up again. His chiselled profile might have been cast in marble. 'I...I a-am s-so sorry,' Chrissy whispered brokenly, devastated that she could have caused so much damage without even the consolation of having achieved something worth while by her deception. Elaine would go ahead with her abortion now.

'I just bet you are,' Elaine derided, triumph emanating from her in waves.

Silent tears trickled down Chrissy's anguished face. Blaze was studying the uneven stone floor. She had hurt him and she had never intended to do that. He had become attached to Rosie so quickly, had been so ready to believe that she was his daughter... and now the humiliating truth had been thrown in his teeth.

'My dear boy... here you both are... This is not the time to weigh anchor. Caught one of those reporter chappies trying to break in through the vestry——'

'I'm afraid there's a hitch,' Elaine announced brightly.

In strong dismay, Chrissy focused on the elderly man in the impressive purple robes and mitre of an Anglican bishop, standing in the entrance to the nave.

Blaze looked at Chrissy, at no one else. She went white. His jewelled eyes were incandescent blue. Not a muscle moved on his darkly handsome visage, but that seething sapphire stare spoke for him. She flinched as though he had struck her. She had grown up with a father who frequently lost his head in temper, but what she felt vibrating from Blaze was infinitely more threatening. It was an explosive black fury far beyond anything her father had ever been able to summon up. Anger, powerful as a physical blow, passionate, savage and dangerously uncontrolled.

Organ music rang out clear, sweet notes into the thundering silence.

'The wedding is off,' Elaine said loudly.

Blaze whipped gracefully round, and suddenly he smiled with breathtaking brilliance. 'Is it?' he drawled in a silky undertone Chrissy had to strain to catch. 'If you could prove to me that your sister had been cavorting with an entire rugby team, I'd only ask her if she enjoyed it. I am insanely in love for the very first time in my life, Elaine, and nothing you can do or say will change that.'

Blinking bemusedly, Chrissy was caught unprepared when a set of fingers with the grip of an iron vice closed round her shoulder.

'Let's get on with it!' Blaze said to the Bishop.

'But... b-but we can't!' Chrissy whispered incredulously as he hauled her, in his godfather's stately wake, to the mouth of the carpeted aisle.

Blaze paid no heed to her protest. The organ music soared into ecstasy. Chrissy, her sister's shattered white face still etched in her mind, attempted to pull free, wildly disconcerted by his extraordinary behaviour. It was over, she had been telling herself sickly, wretchedly, and it shouldn't matter so much to her that it had been Elaine, rather than herself, who had finally broken the bad news.

'Stop it!' he raked at her in a raw aside, giving her a shake. 'You're going through with it. I don't intend to miss out on the grand finale!'

'W-what...?' She was silenced by the astonished stares of the Reverend Mr Haynes and his wife. They had turned to watch them walk up the aisle and had realised that something most peculiar was taking place.

The Bishop was by no means unaware of the same peculiarity. Strangely, though, he chose to ignore it. 'Dearly beloved,' he began in a breathless rush, and from there he went into a trot and then an all-out gallop like a man running the race of his life.

Chrissy was shaking all over, white as snow. Blaze was practically holding her up with that same imprisoning, strong arm. Her thready responses were pried and dredged from her by Blaze's seething glares of expectancy. And then it was over. His godfather was a whiter shade of pale, perspiration beading his brow. As she signed her name, Blaze's hand steadied her wrist.

The Bishop said something about marriage being a road strewn with many rocks, but perseverance and commitment and mutual tolerance, he asserted, would clear a path through an avalanche.

'Smile!' Blaze instructed as he pulled her out on to the church steps.

Tremulously she smiled. She was fathoms deep in shock. She couldn't believe that he had forced her to go through with the ceremony. She couldn't believe that they were actually married. Cameras went off all around them. Had he done it purely to revenge himself on Elaine? Elaine had visibly shrunk away from him when he'd said that he loved her kid sister.

Or was it that fierce pride which had driven him? Didn't he realise that if the marriage hadn't taken place she would have been the one to look a fool, not he? People would just have laughed rather unkindly and said that Blaze Kenyon wasn't the marrying type and hadn't they always known that?

He hauled her through the crush. He smiled, fended off questions, shook hands, stuffed offerings of flowers into Chrissy's nerveless hands. It was rather like being royalty. For a few heady minutes, she was bathed in the golden light of Blaze's popularity, and then the light went out as, shedding confetti everywhere, she was unceremoniously thrust into the Ferrari.

As they drove off, she waited sickly for the first wave of verbal attack. It didn't come. The silence seethed. He headed for the motorway. The silence grew and expanded until it banged like a drumbeat all around her. But still he said nothing. He drove as though the devil himself were chasing them. She kept on waiting for a police siren but it didn't come. Finally, when she simply couldn't bear the silence a second longer, she broke into speech.

'I lied to Elaine because she was p-pregnant! She was going to have an abortion. I th-thought that if I could convince her that R-Rosie was yours——'

Blaze murmured something unrepeatable.

Valiantly, Chrissy continued, 'I thought she would go back to Steve and the b-baby would be safe. I n-never dreamt that she'd tell you what I'd said! And w-when you confronted me, I kept it up because if I hadn't you would have t-told her it was a lie and she would have gone on with the t-termination... Are you l-listening to me?' she prompted pleadingly. 'It was n-never meant to go this far... I am so s-sorry...'

'You're not now, but you will be...' Blaze promised.

He wasn't listening; she knew he wasn't listening. Sheer blinding rage was an exclusive emotion. She sensed that all that existed for Blaze at this precise moment was what she had done. He wasn't interested in the whys and hows. He was centred on the lies, the outrageous, utterly inexcusable deception of allowing him to believe that he had taken gross advantage of a teenage girl, and the equally monstrous duplicity of allowing him to believe that Rosie was his daughter.

Falling silent, she wondered where they were going and asked.

'London,' he said with bite.

'But R-Rosie——!'

'This was arranged in advance. Floss has all sorts of treats planned for her this weekend,' he divulged fiercely.

And presumably he was prepared to go through the motions for the sake of appearances. Guilty colour burned her cheeks. 'I h-have no clothes...'

'You won't be seeing daylight for the rest of the weekend,' Blaze assured her icily. 'Hamish was to bring Rosie down on Monday morning in time for our flight to Paris, but I am not taking you to Paris now.'

Hot, stupid tears scorched her eyelids. Bravely, she forced them back. A honeymoon. He had actually arranged one, albeit a slightly unusual one with Rosie in tow. Dear heaven, she felt so awful, so eaten by remorse and shame. 'I w-wouldn't expect you to——'

'You can switch out of the meek and mild, butter-wouldn't-melt-in-my-rosebud-mouth routine, *right now*!' he cut in rawly. 'At least grant me the intelligence to know when I've been ripped off by a professional! I just can't believe that I fell for it... Guy said, "Check this out, go for the DNA tests, hire a private investigator to dig into your past...deny everything, admit nothing until you are forced." That was his expert advice. And what did I do?' He vented a ferocious laugh. 'I believed you... I felt guilty...I didn't want to humiliate you...I thought you'd already gone through enough. To think that I thought you were different from all the rest——'

'Please!' she sobbed.

'The more you cry, the more I like it...so go ahead,' he said with complete and crushing contempt. 'But keep something back for later, sweetheart. You'll need it. I intend to make you beg and I want a full performance. I want to see those big green eyes swimming with tears and reproach for real *this time*!'

'I'm sorry!' she gasped between sobs. 'Why d-did you f-force me to go through with the marriage? W-why?'

'Why?' His wide mouth hardened. 'You'll find out soon enough.'

Chrissy didn't like the sound of that. She made a huge effort to overcome the tears he had derided, and when the silence, now mercifully welcome, continued she succeeded. He would have the marriage annulled. She fingered the crushed flowers still on her lap and anguish threatened her regained composure.

'Dump those!' Blaze reached ruthlessly for the flowers when he stopped for petrol.

'No!' Chrissy objected, piling them out of his reach.

He had taken a suite at the Savoy. It was beautiful. Her eyes misted over again and she hurriedly moved over to the window to conceal her vulnerability.

'I ordered a complete new wardrobe for you. It should be in the dressing-room. Go and get changed . . . get out of that bloody stupid dress!' Blaze shot at her with raking savagery.

Chrissy spun round. 'I l-like it!' she said defiantly, aware of what he was trying to do. He wanted to destroy all the physical evidence of the marriage that had taken place.

He crossed the width of carpet separating them and, before she could even guess his intention, he hooked a powerful hand into the fragile fabric and ripped it down the front. Chrissy was shocked rigid. Wide-eyed, she linked her arms over the thrust of her exposed breasts.

'If you don't take it off, I'll rip it off,' Blaze drawled lethally.

Trembling, she stood there as he uncrossed her arms, slid the ruined remnants of the dress from her shoulders, and let it fall to her feet. She was literally afraid to move. Then she started to back away in the direction of the bedroom for the clothes he had mentioned. A lean hand yanked her back. 'Why bother? I like the view the way it is.'

Her face crimsoned. Blaze's eyes were incandescent blue again. She had the sinking feeling that the more flesh he saw, the more angry he would become. He slid a deft hand to her narrow back and released her bra, trailing it off, casting it aside. Covering her breasts, she leapt away from him and fled into the bedroom, certain that there had to be a lock on the bathroom door.

She didn't make it. Blaze barred her passage. He was frightening her, really frightening her. She backed away from him, intimidated by the sheer height and breadth of him.

'Cut the comedy act,' he advised, slinging his jacket and tie aside on a chair. 'You don't have a modest bone in your lying, cheating little body. And it's my bet that you're as much of a whore as your sister . . . after all, you have the same groupie tendencies. But you're much cleverer, aren't you?' Diamond-hard blue eyes glittered over her in a brutally male sexual assessment. 'You were damned careful not to get into my bed before we made it to the church. There's a name for women like you, and it isn't a very pleasant one . . .'

Chrissy was shattered by his character-reading. Clearly, he believed nothing that she had told him. Once a liar, always a liar, she reminded herself painfully. He no longer trusted her. He believed she had been playing the tease quite deliberately to fuel his interest. Her stomach twisted sickly. 'I'm not l-like that!'

'No?' An ebony brow elevated in grim, mocking disbelief. He strode out to the lounge and reappeared with a champagne bucket and two glasses. Expertly, he opened the bottle and filled the glasses without spilling a drop. 'So,' he murmured silkily, 'tell me again about how we made love on the floor . . . Refresh my memory.'

The invitation not unnaturally silenced her.

'I didn't take my clothes off . . . is that right?' Blaze prompted in a tone as soft as black velvet. 'And I believe you said it didn't last very long. A rather unnecessary detail, that, wasn't it?'

Chrissy stared at him like an animal in a trap. 'You know now that it n-never happened!'

'Do I? You see, I'm having this inexplicable problem in separating the facts from the fiction. Are you telling me that I never actually laid a finger upon you?'

'Yes,' she confirmed in a driven rush, eager for any excuse to explain and keep him at a distance.

'Really? So I didn't cruelly satisfy my lust on your nubile teenage body and then tell you to get out?'

She bowed her head in embarrassment. 'All...all you did was kiss me and then you p-pushed me away,' she admitted. 'You accused me of...of th-throwing myself at you and then you said th-things about Elaine. You absolutely h-humiliated me; you were unbelievably cruel...'

'Savaged all those tender teenage feelings, did I?'

'I d-didn't throw myself at you!' Even in the midst of a far more serious crisis, that accusation still rankled.

'So, I've never actually had you.' A smile of breath-taking insolence skimmed his wide, sensual mouth. 'That should add a little spice to a weekend in which I intend to have you every which way I can...and I should warn you, your imagination is at the starting stakes in comparison with mine!'

Chrissy's tongue snaked out to moisten her dry lips. He couldn't mean that. Only if the marriage was un-consummated could he apply for an annulment, and the very last thing he would want to do in these circumstances was deprive himself of that escape clause.

'You're wrong,' he drawled as if she had spoken her thoughts out loud. 'I don't care what this weekend costs me.'

'Blaze, I tried to tell you the t-truth before Elaine appeared!' she argued in desperation. 'I would have told you l-last night if you'd come back! You were never meant to know about that lie... It was for Elaine's benefit. She was planning to have a t-termination because she was convinced that she had a future with you. I couldn't let that happen, not when I knew that you were only after revenge!'

'Very impressive. You lie so convincingly.' He awarded her a slow handclap of sardonic applause. 'Little Miss Martyr, in fact...with not a single self-seeking motive of her own in mind——'

'What m-motive could I have?' she demanded weakly. 'I couldn't hope to conceal Rosie's parentage from you indefinitely——'

'No? With the money I have, I'm quite sure that as my wife you would have contrived to find someone somewhere to forge a suitable birth certificate, naming you as her mother. That would have been all you needed to do. I was unlikely to demand blood tests *after* the wedding!'

His clipped, icy delivery rang with the cool of complete conviction. Numbly shaking her head, Chrissy looked at him in appalled silence. He thought she had used Rosie to trap him into marriage.

'And I'd never have known...'

'I'd never h-have done that to you!' she muttered strickenly.

'You're preaching to the converted, sweetheart.' Blaze drained his glass of champagne and studied her with seething intensity, his mouth narrowed to a hard line. 'You're a cheap, calculating little opportunist, and the one thing I am not interested in is the sound of your voice.'

Setting down the glass, he closed the gap between them and she started to breathe fast, reacting to the danger flares in the atmosphere. 'No,' she said with a shiver of fear. 'N-no...'

'It's called paying the piper, Chrissy, and you are going to pay and keep on paying until I get bored with the lack of variety in the entertainment,' he swore.

Lean, terrifyingly strong fingers forced her arms away from her breasts. 'This shrinking, almost virginal modesty is being heavily overplayed,' he censured with hard amusement. 'You're no innocent and I am randy as hell.'

His intent gaze lingered on the pouting breasts he had uncovered and a deep flush carmined her skin, scorching tears lashing her lowered eyelids. 'You c-can't!' she suddenly burst out.

'Rosie may not be mine,' he bit out with whiplash resonance, 'but you are!'

'Blaze, please...' she pleaded, terrified of the idea of him making love to her in the mood he was in.

'All mine...to do exactly as I want with.' He swept her up and dropped her down on the bed without warning. Before she could move out of reach, he had peeled off her briefs and tights with one deft tug.

He followed her down on to the mattress in one lithe movement. 'No need to be coy now, sweetheart,' he murmured, pinning her flat and staring down at her. 'You have really beautiful breasts...and no doubt I'm not the first man to tell you that!'

Turmoil in her distressed eyes, Chrissy looked up at him, her throat convulsing. His dark head angled down and he ran the tip of his tongue tauntingly across the panting upswell of her breasts on his path to a rosy nipple. She went rigid, fighting the jerk of instant sensation with all her might.

'It won't work... You're just as desperate for this as I am,' Blaze told her harshly.

She flinched, shut her eyes tightly, determined to behave like a block of wood, and then maybe he would leave her alone. But she trembled when he shaped her breasts with his hands, shivered when he teased her with his tongue and his teeth, and dug both hands into the bedding to prevent herself making a shameless grab for him when he invaded her mouth with devastating expertise.

'Don't,' she gasped against that assault, for she knew he was powered by contempt and a desire to humiliate her and to respond to such a calculated onslaught would be an inexcusable self-betrayal.

She could feel her breasts swelling almost painfully beneath his palms, her heart racing to a mad, accelerated peak, outside her control. And she knew that he had already won, because her hunger for him was surging through her in great waves of abandonment. Everything that had gone before fell into limbo. His mouth was back on her breasts and tortured gasps escaped her as he stroked and circled and tormented the hard, puckered nubs he had already roused to unbearable sensitivity.

The rough, curling hair on his chest scratched her satin-smooth stomach and she arched and ached all in one involuntary movement beneath him, her thighs trembling with the raw depth of her arousal.

Abruptly, she was freed, and she let a stifled sound of protest flee her lips before she opened her eyes. Blaze was discarding what remained of his clothing and when he returned to her she shivered as she came into contact with his muscled thighs and then she felt the full force of his arousal, hot and smooth and hard against her. Heat pooled instantly in her pelvis.

She was making the discovery that she wanted to touch and explore him too. Her fingers laced into the hair on his broad chest, smoothed over his brown skin, tracing the taut lines of his ribcage as his breath came in increasingly audible pants. She freed her mouth to find a muscular shoulder sheathed in silky smooth skin that she caressed with her tongue, then nipped daringly with her teeth, having learnt fast from the lessons he had unwittingly given her.

He twisted his head and took her mouth again, roughly, urgently, and the most ferocious tension snaked her every muscle taut. She didn't want to stay still...it was impossible to stay still as his hand explored between her parted thighs. She moaned low in her throat, a disturbingly animal sound, her limbs trembling, her back arching in jerky, uncontrolled movements.

'You are so small...so tight,' he groaned and he murmured other things, wild, arousingly intimate assurances of exactly how he was going to make her feel.

She was literally mindless with desire when he tipped her up, spreading her legs wide and high as he came down on her. Her entire body was centred on the raw ache of need eating her up. She was writhing, shaking, entirely mastered by that hunger when she felt his probing hardness surge against her and instinctively tensed.

'Don't...' Blaze groaned, his hands forcing her still as he entered her degree by painful degree.

It hurt like hell and she cried out as he thrust deep into her soft sheath, rending the flimsy barrier that had sought to deny him. With a raw sound of all-male satisfaction, he took full possession.

Only then did he pause, sapphire-blue eyes bright with astonishment as he raked her pale, tense face. 'Rosie would indeed have been a miracle... No wonder you didn't dare let me this close,' he breathed with uninhibited satisfaction, slumbrous and entirely unexpected amusement gleaming from his piercing gaze as he moved on her in an almost taunting reminder of his sexual supremacy.

'Stop it!'

'I love it,' he murmured provocatively. 'You lie and you cheat but basically you're just a nice girl, who very properly saved herself for her husband. I am truly grateful for an experience I never thought to have. Relax; I'll be gentle but I am not going to stop...'

She absolutely hated him at that instant. But a second later he found her mouth in a series of soft, tormentingly brief kisses, and the fire, doused by pain, began, incredibly, to flame again. She told herself that she couldn't want this to continue, but her body taught her different, trembling and suddenly melting beneath his slow, careful thrusts. Her head fell back, her breathing ruptured as the pleasure began to build to unbearable extremes.

'Shall I stop?' Blaze whispered mockingly.

'No...' she gasped, on the brink of a rolling wave of ecstasy that went on and on, taking her to unbelievable heights. She could no longer fight her own emotions, her own natural instincts, and she moved with him, went leaping off that highest pinnacle of sensation in the belief that she could fly as he shuddered into climax above her.

Releasing her, he threw himself back against the pillows, leaving her feeling completely bereft as she fell back down through the cotton-wool clouds of satiation to the hard realities of life. The silence was the reality. She must have imagined that glorious feeling of bonding on a higher plane when he'd made love to her.

The mattress gave with his departure. She listened to him running a bath in the *en suite*. She felt like a victim who had wantonly and stupidly participated in her own downfall. In the field of sexual experience, she was a mere beginner, and his incredulous amusement had hurt. After telling her exactly what he thought of her, he had forced her into bed to play to the full the role of a bride on her wedding night. And, in doing that, he had humiliated her by effortlessly asserting his sexual dominance. She felt used and abused and bitter and miserable and thoroughly sorry for herself.

The bedding was trailed unceremoniously back before she could make a grab for it. Blaze lifted her and then paused to stare in shock at the evidence of her lost innocence plainly visible on the sheet. He went pale. 'My God,' he breathed. 'I think you need a doctor... Are you supposed to bleed like——?'

It was the last straw. Flooded by raw mortification, Chrissy struck out at him with a flailing fist. 'You sadist!' she shrieked.

He ducked the blow and, striding into the *en suite*, he gently lowered her down into the soothing heat of the bath he had filled. 'If I were a real sadist,' he said smoothly, 'I would be following my natural inclinations and you would still be in that bed. I wouldn't give a damn how much I was hurting you. So don't tempt fate. After all, out of bed, I don't have much use for you!'

The door thudded closed and she burst into tears, stifling the sound behind her shaking hands. She had known that, but somehow, until it was unashamedly slung at her, she had been able to shelter from that most agonising truth. More than anything else in the world, she wanted him to care for her just a little, even the way he had before. Right now, she wasn't too proud to accept that as the most she was likely to receive.

But even that was out of reach, she sensed wretchedly. She had dug her own grave with Blaze. He didn't trust her, he didn't like her and he certainly had no respect for her. She had lied and this was her punishment. Permitting herself the indulgence of weak tears was pathetic, she told herself. Tears would change nothing. Elaine would go home to Steve and Chrissy couldn't even congratulate herself on that count. Blaze would have contrived that miracle all by himself and without any assistance from her.

CHAPTER TEN

CHRISSY climbed out of the car and walked into the house. Rosie charged at her and gave her an excited hug, but one second later she asked, 'Blaze?'

'Blaze is b-busy, pet.' Chrissy hurriedly turned to speak to Floss.

'It's a crying shame you couldn't go to Paris. Men!' Floss grumbled. 'As if the yard couldn't survive without him for a week! With the builders still here, the yard is only running at half its capacity. I think you should have put your foot down——'

'I don't mind,' Chrissy put in, alert to the sound of Blaze's footsteps in the hall.

'Oh, before I forget... I was talking to Phyllis Roper, who runs the playgroup in the village. She said they might have a place for Rosie...'

The moment that Chrissy was most dreading arrived as Rosie scrambled off her lap at speed and headed for Blaze like a homing pigeon.

As Rosie intercepted him at the foot of the stairs, he froze, his brilliant blue eyes veiled, his strikingly handsome features clenching hard as Rosie wrapped both arms round his knees, innocently demanding the welcome she had learnt to expect from him. For a split-second he looked so intensely alone that Chrissy's throat ached.

'Blaze—Daddy,' Rosie enunciated quite clearly, and Chrissy's cup of poison truly overflowed.

'It just slipped out once,' Floss confided worriedly, 'and ever since I said it she's been saying it. I'm sorry.'

'No problem,' Blaze drawled flatly, but the look he directed at Chrissy was like a knife thudding into a target.

'Time I was getting on... No, there's no need to see me out,' Floss insisted.

Chrissy had the mobility of a statue. Everything that Blaze had refused to talk about over the weekend was in that scorching blue stare of bitter condemnation. Rosie... And Rosie was not something Blaze wished to discuss. She had let him believe that Rosie was his child and, now that he was faced with Rosie again, knowing the truth, Chrissy's damaging deception was once more laid bare.

Unexpectedly, he gave way to the toddler's pleas and bent down and lifted her up. Certain that he couldn't want that contact, Chrissy hurried forward. 'Let m-me take h-her,' she urged miserably.

'You bitch,' Blaze whispered. 'You absolute bitch.'

Chrissy fell back as though she had been struck, every remaining scrap of colour evaporating from her drawn cheeks. Both arms wrapped protectively around Rosie, Blaze stared down at Chrissy with unconcealed loathing and distaste.

Dazed and sick, she swayed into the kitchen and sank down weakly at the table. How could he have made love to her when he felt like that? Were men so different in temperament? The weekend had been an exercise in humiliation, executed with ruthless cool and precision. In two days, she had not once left that suite.

He had ordered dinner to be served up there that first night. Then he had simply walked out after the meal. She didn't know where, hadn't had the guts to ask. She had gone to bed, and graciously he had allowed her to sleep in peace. But between breakfast the following morning and lunch forty-eight hours later when they checked out, Blaze had kept her almost continuously in the bedroom. Her pale complexion flamed at the snatches of erotic imagery indelibly printed on her memory. He was an insatiable lover.

Blaze had instinctively known what would hurt her most. Time and time again, he had made her lose control in his arms, and that loss of control had tortured her when she knew that he wanted to make her feel like the racetrack groupies he had compared her to...the women who hung around the track, willing to sleep with any man who was *someone* in the racing world, the women drawn by the fame, the money and the excitement that were all part of his existence.

He had told her that he didn't have any use for her out of bed and he had driven home the message with humiliating ease. And maybe she could have liked herself better had she found it possible to switch off the instantaneous leap of shameless response that controlled her every time he touched her. Even if she had managed that once, she thought with bitter self-loathing. He had savaged her self-respect. What sort of a woman was she that she could respond to a male who made no secret of his hatred for her?

He strolled into the kitchen. She didn't look at him. She was afraid to look, terrified that her wildly fluctuating emotions would betray her. He didn't know that she had been stupid enough to fall in love with him, and the thought of what he was likely to do with that piece of information made her blood ice up in her veins. He already had more than enough ammunition to hurt her. She shrank from the prospect of that wickedly derisive tongue of his shredding her most private emotions. He would laugh at her, she knew he would . . . and she didn't think she could bear that.

'I heard Floss mentioning the playgroup in the village. You should get down there and enrol Rosie,' he drawled.

Chrissy tensed, complete incomprehension sweeping over her as it had so often over the weekend. He talked as if they were staying . . . but for how long?

'What would be the p-point?' she muttered.

'She ought to be mixing with other children. It's lonely up here for her.'

'We're not g-going to be here f-forever.'

'But you are here now——'

'You c-can't want us here!' she suddenly burst out helplessly.

'For as long as I want you warming my bed every night, you're staying,' he delivered without a flicker of conscience.

Tears springing to her eyes, she watched the table surface haze out of focus, that familiar choking sensation closing over her throat. In despair, she fought to control the tears. Tears made him angry. Anger made him derisive. Derision cut her to the bone. Her hands were shaking and she braced them hard on the scarred wood. 'I c-can't live like this,' she admitted jerkily.

'Three days of marriage and you're a basket case.' Blaze stroked a taunting forefinger over one of her unsteady hands. 'I hate to state the obvious, but isn't this what you wanted? To be Mrs Blaze Kenyon? Rich, secure... and, if not loved, sexually satisfied?'

Chrissy tugged her hand out of reach but, even though he was no longer touching her, she was painfully aware of his proximity with every fibre in her body. 'No! I w-would never have gone through w-with the wedding——'

'Forgive me if I continue to find that assertion unbelievable——'

'I swear I was about to t-tell you! I was... I w-was,' she argued feverishly, but at the back of her mind loomed a disturbing recall of the way in which she had fallen silent in the church vestibule when he'd murmured that she was *so* pretty in pink. For a split-second, she had fatally hesitated because she had known in that instant how very badly she did want it all to be real. For that split-second, she had wanted to marry him, had wanted Rosie to be his... and the awareness of that fact tortured her now. Did that make her guilty as charged?

'I'm eating down at the Pheasant tonight.' He strode out of the door.

She was asleep when she heard the slam of the front door. She peered at the luminous dial on her alarm clock.

It was after twelve. Where had he been until this hour? Her bedroom door opened abruptly.

'What are you doing in here?' Blaze enquired drily.

'Trying to sleep,' she mumbled.

'But not in my bed.' Chillingly cold blue eyes bit into her.

It was on the tip of her tongue to say that sleep was the last thing she was likely to get in that location, but she swallowed it back. It had not even occurred to her that she would be expected to take up residence in his bedroom. Still sleepy, she said so.

'Bloody hell,' he grated with sudden unexpected ferocity. 'We're married!'

'Are w-we?' she dared, with an air of surprise. 'You see, I thought that c-ceremony on Friday was just your passport to a dirty weekend...'

'And yours,' he batted back without pause, 'considering that you carefully withheld all favours until you got that ring firmly stuck on your finger.'

She reddened fiercely.

In the interim, he scooped her out of her nice, comfy bed, sent a very familiar hand skimming possessively over a slender hip, and murmured smoothly, 'So go warm up my bed, sweetheart. I paid in advance...'

Chrissy spun round, flushed with absolute outrage. 'I won't l-let you treat me like some kind of tramp!'

A powerful hand anchored itself to her wrist. He trailed her down the corridor and thrust her into his bedroom. Uneasily aware of the flimsy nature of her silk nightdress, she climbed into the bed.

'But I am treating you the same way you treated me,' Blaze drawled, sinking down with innate grace into an armchair in the corner and stretching out his long legs in an attitude of predatory relaxation. 'Without the slightest consideration for your feelings...'

Chrissy lowered her eyes, the angry colour ebbing from her face. She *had* treated him that way. On that charge, she had no defence to offer. She would never forget how

desperately alone he had looked in that split-second when
Rosie had grabbed him. It had hurt Chrissy to be a
witness to that pain. She had not foreseen that vulnerability, but she should have done. In many ways, Blaze
had been alone all his life.

'You hurt me... It's been a long time since anyone
managed to do that,' he said almost conversationally.
'So long, I had forgotten when it felt like. I don't get
close to people, but I got close to Rosie...'

Moisture was gritting her eyelids. Wretchedly, she just
nodded her head in acknowledgement, unable to meet
his direct gaze. She hadn't been prepared for him to
admit that he had been hurt. The blunt admission shook
her up even more.

'Before she came along, I had never had anything to
do with children... at least not one as young as that.
She's so trusting, so sweet... When you told me she was
mine, maybe part of me wanted to believe it...'

'I know.' Chrissy was more ashamed than ever.

'How long have you been with her?'

'Practically since she was born... Mum couldn't cope
very well,' Chrissy admitted. 'I was at college, but I used
to come home and find Rosie c-crying, not changed,
maybe not fed. It was as if Mum could forget she was
there. It worried me sick, so in the end I dropped out
of my course...'

'And you ended up taking over?'

'She told me once th-that Dennis was furious when
she told him she was pregnant. And you see, she only
g-got pregnant for him... because he was younger and
she thought he would want a child.' Chrissy's tremulous
mouth hardened. 'But, of course, he didn't, and by then
he had run through most of her divorce settlement. He
was treating her pretty badly long before he walked out
on her. When he was arrested and the police came to
question her, she was absolutely shattered and she didn't
tell them that she was pregnant... She was ashamed of
it. She just never got over that...'

'Why did you keep Rosie after she died?' he prompted almost lazily.

Chrissy looked up in genuine surprise. 'Because I love her...'

His sensual mouth hardened. 'Is that why you pretended she was mine...for her benefit?'

Her brow creased in dismay. 'No! I l-lied to Elaine, not you——'

'You lied to me,' he cut in chillingly.

'Only because I didn't w-want Elaine to have an abor——'

'I don't want to hear that nonsense again!' Blaze sprang upright and strode to the foot of the bed. 'Elaine isn't pregnant and she isn't about to have an abortion,' he asserted with savage coldness. 'I want the truth, not some stupid, childish story!'

'It is the t-truth.' Her head was pounding. 'But I c-can't prove it to you...'

'Have you got legal custody of Rosie?' he demanded abruptly.

Chrissy stared at him. 'No.'

'Well, that is good to know,' Blaze drawled smoothly, 'considering that you are totally unfit to have custody of an impressionable child——'

'What do y-you know?' Desperately hurt and distressed by the condemnation, Chrissy shouted back at him. 'I've done my b-best!'

'But your best hasn't been good enough for her or for me.' Blaze sent her a glittering look of derision. 'You are a liar and I can't stand liars. I can't trust anything you say.'

Anger gave her the strength to fight him. Blaze had started the deception, hadn't he? His desire for revenge had given birth to this entire situation, and Blaze hadn't given a damn who was hurt!

'You talk as if everything is my fault,' she condemned. 'But you brought Rosie and me up here to use us... You weren't concerned about people assuming that she was your child then ... You didn't care what they said about me or her as long as it embarrassed my father!'

'You were drowning and I threw you a lifeline.'

'That's not the p-point——'

'You had no other options and you must have known what people would think.'

'I was s-so grateful for the job, it didn't even occur to me until it was too late,' she argued starkly. 'But you set me up——'

'How?'

'The very first morning you sent one of the stable girls up to collect that c-case, knowing that I was still in your bed!'

A sardonic brow quirked. 'Rubbish. I'd actually forgotten you were there.'

'Taking me t-to the Pheasant ... that was deliberate,' she accused in growing desperation.

'Bloody hell ...' he breathed with outright derision. 'I took you there so that you could have a bath.'

'Really?'

'And if you had got out of that bath and into the bed with me...well,' he conceded with insolent cool, 'I wasn't about to object. Frankly, your family were the last thing on my mind that afternoon.'

Chrissy buried her burning cheeks in a pillow, stiff with defeat.

'The one time when I might have caused you actual harm was three years ago,' Blaze drawled. 'And I didn't. I never blamed you for what your father and your sister did ...'

She hated to admit it, but that was true. Sticks and stones didn't break your bones. He could have devastated her that night by telling her what her family had done to his grandfather, but he hadn't. He could have blamed her, but he hadn't.

Curling up into a tight ball, she turned her back on him, steeped in despair. A bitch, he had called her, an absolute bitch, and he couldn't stand liars. Well, she couldn't stand to share a bed with someone who thought about her in those terms!

She listened tautly to the sound of him undressing. He reached for her and pulled her across the bed into his arms. She went rigid. 'D-don't touch me...don't you d-dare!'

'Lie back and think martyred thoughts,' Blaze advised callously. 'A woman tried to chat me up tonight in the Pheasant...'

If possible, Chrissy went even more rigid. 'W-what?'

'And I suddenly remembered that I had a wife at home...a wife who went to incredible lengths to get me. But since we are married...' a lean hand closed suggestively round one pouting breast '...I might as well take full advantage of what you might call the facilities.'

'No!' she said fiercely, and for the first time she really fought him. He laughed, dispensed with her nightdress in a breathless struggle that she lost within minutes, and captured both her flailing hands in one of his, pinning them to the pillow above her head.

Sapphire-blue eyes gleamed down into wild green ones. 'Surrender?'

'I hate you! I'll n-never forgive you for what you said about Rosie,' she threw back bitterly, painfully. 'Just g-get it over with and leave me alone!'

'If that's what you want...'

Afterwards, she knew that it hadn't been, lying there in the darkness with tears sliding down her cheeks while she listened to his even breathing on the other side of the bed. He hadn't even kissed her. She hadn't known that making love could be like that, that she could be made to feel the way she felt now. It had been an act of sex, stripped of all things tender and pleasurable. He hadn't hurt her, he had just...just... How could he do that? He had entered her body and taken his own pleasure with a cold efficiency that shattered her. An act he had previously contrived to make special...something she hadn't appreciated until much too late...had suddenly become the most gross invasion of privacy, the most utter humiliation.

She was downstairs before he was the next morning. Breakfast was served without a single word on her part. They couldn't go on like this...*she* couldn't go on like this, she realised miserably, listening to him respond to Rosie's chatter without a shade of irritation. She had been afraid that he would take his anger out on the toddler and reject her. Once again, she had misjudged him. Yet somehow his continuing kindness towards Rosie didn't make her feel any better. It simply seemed to emphasise her own isolation.

Blaze hated her now. She just wasn't strong enough to bear that day in, day out. The anger, the taunts, the derision, the tension. He was breaking her down piece by piece. Sooner or later, he would bring her to her knees. It hurt too much to face that she had brought all of this on herself. She had given him a very big stick to beat her with and he was not averse to causing pain. She had always known how cruel he could be, but for a while she had stood within a charmed circle. Now she was outside that circle...and that hurt... Dear lord, but that hurt.

Abruptly, she grabbed Rosie's hand and went to get her jacket. She had to get out of the house to sort out the turmoil of her own emotions.

'Where are you going?'

Chrissy stilled. 'Do y-you know where the playgroup is held?'

'Church hall, I should think. Can I trust you not to bolt?'

Chrissy sent him an embittered look, her tense shoulders drooping in sudden defeat. Distressed green eyes collided with brilliant blue ones. 'Where would I go?'

*   *   *

At the playgroup, Rosie left her side within ten minutes.

'If I were you, I'd take off,' Phyllis Roper advised cheerfully. 'If she gets upset, we'll bring her home, but she seems quite confident, doesn't she? Not that that proves anything. You never know how they'll react until you actually leave them.'

Chrissy was climbing back into the Discovery when a car shot to a screeching halt by the railings. A man vaulted out at speed and her eyes narrowed in dismay. It was her brother-in-law. That shock of curly auburn hair teamed with a beard was quite unmistakable. One hand on the steering-wheel, she watched him stride towards her, a tall, burly man in a rather shabby suit.

'I think we need to talk, Chrissy,' he breathed tightly. 'Or maybe commiserate would be a better word...'

She was shocked by the harsh lines of strain etched into his set features. Without asking permission, he settled himself into the passenger seat beside her and then he sat like someone in a daze, simply staring silently out of the windscreen.

'I'm sorry.' He sighed, with an obvious effort to pull himself together. 'I am so sorry that you've got mixed up in this as well.'

To say that Chrissy was stricken by his appearance was to put it mildly. It was obvious that Steve had come down to see Elaine. That meant that Elaine had not, as Chrissy had hoped, gone home yet. Furthermore, Steve's visible stress indicated that, if he had had a meeting with his errant wife, that meeting had gone badly. She dropped her head, thinking fast. How much did Steve know about what had been happening down here? The last thing Chrissy wanted to do was make matters worse by being indiscreet.

'You've seen Elaine...' she gathered awkwardly.

'I came down to bring her home.' Steve vented a harsh laugh. 'I thought this was just another one of her tantrums. God knows, I wonder sometimes why I even want her back...'

'You love her——'

'Do you love him? The bastard, the lousy rotten bastard!' Steve suddenly bit out viciously without warning. 'Is this how he gets his kicks? Doesn't he care who gets hurt? I could have fought anybody but him...anybody!' he swore with aggression, as if Chrissy was about to argue with him. 'But I don't look like a bloody movie star and I'm not rich and the only time I ever got on a horse I landed flat on my face in the mud!'

'C-calm down, Steve,' Chrissy pleaded, out of her depth. Dear lord, how much did he know? What had Elaine told him?

Abruptly, he drove an unsteady hand through his hair and drew in a deep, shaking breath. 'He'd never do anything that crass, would he...your precious husband?' he spelt out. 'He's so perfect, he's inhuman, but he's got the moral restraint of a tomcat and you must have known that when you married him!'

'Steve——'

'So what I'm about to tell you can't come as any real surprise,' Steve asserted tightly, one big hand clenched in a fist on his thigh. 'Elaine never got over him... She married me on the rebound and, if I'm honest, I was glad enough to take her on those terms...'

Chrissy took her troubled eyes from his working profile and looked away. Dear heaven, had Blaze ever once thought about how all this would affect Elaine's husband? Had he even cared? True, Elaine had left Steve to come down and throw herself in Blaze's path again, but it had been his encouragement that made her stay.

'I knew what she was doing when she came down here,' Steve continued grimly. 'But I thought he'd tell her to get lost...'

'He h-has...'

'I'm sorry, Chrissy...' He released his breath heavily. 'She was going to come home with me—I'm certain she was—and then the phone rang. I eavesdropped. It was him...'

Chrissy tried and failed to swallow. 'Blaze? Blaze ph-phoned Elaine? When?'

'About half an hour ago. If we sit here long enough, you'll see him driving past on his way over there. She couldn't get me out the door fast enough,' Steve related harshly, painfully. 'So you tell me... If he hates her, what's going on?'

Chrissy was fumbling nervelessly with the key in the ignition.

'He married you not four days ago, and the second you're out of sight he goes to Elaine,' Steve spelt out unnecessarily.

'Would you mind g-getting out of the car?'

'What the——?' Steve frowned at her and then reached for her hand. 'Chrissy, let them get on with it. They deserve each other——'

'I'll k-kill him!' Chrissy spat back.

'That's how I felt,' Steve muttered wearily. 'But what's the point?'

'The p-point, Steve, is that h-he is my husband!' Chrissy exclaimed. 'Now get out of the c-car!'

Her brother-in-law shook his head. 'You'll only humiliate yourself if you confront him——'

'L-like h-hell I w-will!' she stammered fiercely.

Steve climbed out. 'Look, I'll be at the Pheasant until lunchtime. I don't think I should drive, the way I feel right now...'

No such inhibition afflicted Chrissy. She drove off like a rocket heading for outer space. A rage unlike anything she had ever experienced possessed her. How dared Blaze do this to Steve? How dared Blaze approach Elaine again? Hadn't he caused enough trouble? Steve must have made a mistake. It couldn't have been Blaze on the phone, she decided abruptly. She wouldn't put it past her sister to have another man up her sleeve with whom to soothe her battered ego!

Blaze was strolling towards the Ferrari when she screeched to a halt. Not surprisingly, he stilled, an expression of incredulity on his starkly handsome features.

'If that is an example of your driving proficiency,' he drawled, 'you have just lost your wheels. Give me the keys.'

She threw them at him. 'Where are y-you going?'

Blaze scooped up the keys with complete cool. 'I gather Rosie is at the playgroup. When does it finish? I'll pick her up on the way back.'

He hadn't answered her. He was moving towards the Ferrari again. Her belief that Steve had got it all wrong suffered a sudden lurch in confidence. 'Where a-are you going?' she demanded, her tone half an octave higher.

'I'll be back in time for lunch...I think.'

She sprinted across the gravel like a maniac and plastered herself against the driver's door of his car. 'I ran into Steve in the v-village! He told me that you were going to see Elaine...'

'Yes...' Blaze planted two powerful hands to her waist and set her aside, taking full advantage of the shock dealt by that careless affirmative.

It was as if the world had stopped turning. Paralysed by horror, she stared at him. 'But y-you...but you c-can't be...'

'I am,' Blaze bit out with chilling impatience. 'And when I need your permission to go anywhere, I'll be two feet underground, pushing up daisies——'

'I...I won't let you go!' Chrissy shrieked at him. 'I'd sooner y-you were d-dead!'

Dense black lashes dropped low over his intent gaze. He stared at her, sapphire-blue eyes absorbing her trembling, her ferocity, her total abandonment of any form of self-control. Wild green eyes assaulted his in violent threat. Disturbingly he dealt her a sudden brilliant smile. 'Where are the spare keys for the Discovery?' he enquired quietly.

'W-what?'

'Forget it.' In one long stride he had reached her car, flipped open the bonnet, and extracted something. 'I have this strange feeling that commiting adultery with you around could be a considerable challenge...'

Anguish in her eyes, she watched him swing into the Ferrari and drive off. Rage and disbelief were tearing her apart. She couldn't believe that he could just go to Elaine like that! And yet he had, openly, unashamedly, making it brutally clear that neither her feelings nor those of Elaine's husband mattered a damn.

Her head was spinning. Was it possible that in some twisted fashion he really did care about Elaine? Or was he still after revenge? Chrissy didn't know... She didn't feel she was in a fit state to know anything any more. All she knew was that the man she loved was on his way to her far more beautiful sister where he was assured of a rapturous welcome. He hadn't even bothered to lie to her... Evidently he didn't consider her that important.

The truth was agonisingly painful. She wasn't his wife, not in any real sense. Blaze didn't think of her as his wife. She was the home help he slept with. He despised her. He had forced her down that aisle in a rage. She was behaving like a wronged wife and he hadn't given her that status. She hurt all over. Mental pain had somehow become physical as well. He's with Elaine now, she thought, and she wanted to die...

For the first hour she paced the floor. An hour beyond that, drained of all movement, she was lying face down on the bed. She began to panic. Rosie was due out of the playgroup soon and she couldn't believe that Blaze would be there to pick her up. Then she heard the unmistakable low throb of the Ferrari.

She couldn't face going downstairs, couldn't face another confrontation within hearing distance of the yard. She and Rosie would leave Westleigh Hall with dignity, she promised herself, cold, frigid dignity. She heard his light step on the stairs. Rosie had probably gone into the kitchen to find her.

'Rosie's with Floss.'

Chrissy reared up and snatched at the first object that came to hand. Her alarm clock went sailing across the room and smashed harmlessly against the wall. He ducked, though, which gave her some satisfaction. 'You f-filthy womaniser!' she screamed at him. 'I'm leaving y-you!'

'Chance would be a fine thing,' he derided, kicking the door shut in his wake.

He looked incredibly cool, calm and collected. In fact, if it hadn't been beyond the bounds of amusement, she would have sworn that amusement briefly flickered in that sapphire-blue gaze. 'Why didn't you simply tell me that Elaine was pregnant?' he asked with level emphasis.

Her eyes flew wide and she stared at him.

'I really ought to cringe from the image you must have of me.' Blaze sighed. 'I would have backed off from your sister the minute you told me. I certainly wouldn't have wanted an abortion on my conscience...'

In shock, her tongue snaked out to moisten her dry lips. 'Elaine...Elaine admitted th-that she was——'

'With a little persuasion,' Blaze interposed smoothly. 'Why do you think I went over there?

'I...I thought...'

'Rampantly jealous, aren't you?' he mocked. 'It occurred to me that I ought to check your story out...give you the benefit of the doubt just one more time——'

'I was n-not jealous!' Chrissy snapped fierily and then frowned, still struggling to comprehend that he had approached Elaine for the truth. That in itself hurt.

'And now you're angry that I didn't believe you. I'm sorry.' His mouth tautened. 'But whether or not she was pregnant was really quite immaterial. My main reason for going over there was Rosie...'

'R-Rosie?' she echoed in bewilderment.

'I wanted the name of your mother's lawyer. But Elaine told me something that should make adopting Rosie easier...'

Chrissy was entirely lost. 'Adopting h-her?'

'Dennis Carruthers is dead,' Blaze proffered flatly. 'He was killed in a car accident a couple of weeks after he got out on parole.'

'You w-want to adopt Rosie?' Chrissy prompted, not even able to react to the news of Dennis's death.

'Obviously. We'll get in touch with the social services as soon as possible. I want everything on a legal basis,' Blaze stressed gently. 'When Rosie's old enough to understand, we'll tell her the truth about her parentage, but I fully intend to treat her exactly if she were our child.'

'We' and 'our', he had said, indicating that she was expected to play a part in his adoption plans. Chrissy was trembling. 'Blaze...I don't think I kn-know what you're talking about...'

'I have disabused Elaine of the idea that I have any interest in her,' Blaze imparted, drawing closer to the bed. 'I even spent an hour with Steve down at the Pheasant——'

'Steve?' she ejaculated incredulously.

'I told him that absolutely nothing had happened between Elaine and me...'

'Really?' Chrissy responded, painfully unconvinced.

'I have never slept with your sister.' Intensely blue eyes rested on her. 'Three years ago, she got into bed with another man in the belief that it would make me want her more. It didn't... It turned me right off. That's why I ditched her.'

Chrissy stared back at him in stunned surprise. She had always assumed that his relationship with Elaine had been an intimate one. 'You n-never——? I mean——'

'Never.'

Her head was reeling. 'You said you saw Steve...'

'I felt he deserved the truth.' His mouth twisted expressively. 'He's not likely to get much of that from his wife. Elaine had told me that they were in the middle of a divorce—I gather that was quite an exaggeration...'

'Yes.'

Blaze frowned. 'I felt really sorry for the poor bastard. He seems to know what she's like but it doesn't seem to make any difference to him. He talks about her as if she's a spoilt, not very bright child... and I dare say that when he finds out about the baby he'll be delighted. She was in quite a state when I left her... I have this feeling she'll fall on his neck...'

'You were with h-her in London,' Chrissy said tightly. 'What happened?'

'She showed up without invitation.' He dealt her a derisive smile. 'Don't you know that sister of yours? She knew where my apartment was and called in. I took her out to dinner and I agreed to give her a lift home the next morning. That's all it took to play her along and enrage your father.'

'What d-did you do with the killer bimbo while you were down there?' she persisted doggedly.

Faint colour darkened his hard cheekbones. 'If you want me to be frank——'

'Oh, yes,' Chrissy asserted tightly.

'I did plan to go to bed with her, but I didn't. I couldn't get you out of my mind.'

'Am I supposed to believe that?' Chrissy felt achingly vulnerable, and her gaze clung to his dark features. 'Why did you go to see Elaine and Steve?'

He sank down on the edge of the bed. He expelled his breath audibly. 'Last night... I felt like hell afterwards——'

'You w-were asleep——'

'No. Hurting you, I discovered, hurts me,' he drawled flatly. 'Last night, I went too far and I knew I had to sort it all out before I completely blew our relationship...'

'I wasn't aware that we had one,' she muttered tightly, afraid to believe what he was telling her.

'I didn't mean what I said about you being unfit to have Rosie,' he breathed harshly. 'I just wanted to hurt you...'

'Maybe you were right,' she whispered.

'I was totally wrong. You really love her, and that really impressed me from the first moment I saw the two of you together,' Blaze imparted. 'If my mother had had to struggle like that to keep me, I'd have ended up in a children's home...'

Without even thinking about it, Chrissy smoothed a hand over a lean, muscled thigh. 'No...'

'Yes,' he contradicted wryly. 'Giving birth to me was Barb's big rebellion. She didn't realise until it was too late that as far as her contemporaries were concerned she had put herself beyond the pale. If she'd had a discreet termination or gone away and given me up, nobody would have batted an eyelash. But she broke the rules and she was punished for it. My grandfather told me that I had ruined her life——'

'That was wicked!' Chrissy told him hotly.

'Chocolate with a melting centre,' Blaze murmured huskily, tugging her into his arms without warning. 'What did I tell you about men with sob stories?'

Uncertainly she blinked up at him and then her cheeks burned, her slender length already reacting to the hard, masculine angles of his body against hers. He was prepared to forgive her for what she had done because he didn't want to let Rosie go, she reflected painfully. It wasn't enough, it would never be enough... but disturbingly she couldn't find the strength to object when sure hands began peeling off her clothing.

'We sh-shouldn't do this,' she muttered shakily.

'I came back from London one hundred per cent determined to get you into bed,' he confided, pressing his mouth hotly to the sweet valley between her breasts. 'And then you most inconveniently fell down drunk at my feet after telling me that I was everything you didn't want...'

'I th-think I lied.' Chrissy was having great difficulty in concentrating.

'It was like being hit by lightning. I was actually quite grateful that you passed out... That was the moment that I realised I had fallen in love for the first time in my life. I was shattered,' he revealed somewhat indistinctly as his tongue circled the shallow indentation of her navel.

Every muscle jerked taut. Chrissy gave a faint gasp, arching her back. 'Love?'

'It had to be love. I felt like a heel. I'd got you drunk...I had every intention of getting you flat on your back...'

'Had y-you?' She moaned as he travelled perilously close to the tender flesh on the inside of one thigh.

'I'd thought about nothing else for days... I was obsessed with this idea that once I had you I would be able to forget you again...'

'Ah...' The soft bitten-back sigh was forced from her. She could feel control slipping inexorably away. 'Stop talking...'

'And you call me a hedonist,' he murmured provocatively. 'I have just told you that I am madly in love with you and you tell me to shut up!'

Glazed green eyes focused on him incredulously. 'Did I...? Do you?'

'Why do you think I married you?

'You said to Elaine——'

'That I was insanely in love... I must have been to stand her revelation about Rosie and still go ahead.' He uttered a soft, teasing laugh. 'I couldn't let you go. I wanted to strangle you...but I just couldn't let you go. Why do you think I was in such a rage? I told myself I was going to make your life a living hell...'

'I didn't want to tell you the truth at the ch-church,' Chrissy confided in a shamed undertone. 'I wanted you...'

'Sordid lust for my beautiful body.' Blaze groaned with rampant amusement. 'I never thought you'd admit that...'

'I love you!' Chrissy argued fierily.

Raw heat pooled in the pit of her stomach as he ground his lean hips erotically into the cradle of her thighs. His blatant arousal electrified her. Laughing sapphire-blue eyes swept over her hectically flushed face. 'You're just ashamed that you haven't got better taste.'

'I have superb taste,' Chrissy asserted with a certain degree of smugness, lost in a state of positive bliss.

He took her mouth with devouring hunger and the world spun violently on its axis. A very, very long time later, when she had come down from the clouds, she murmured, 'I really am sorry that I lied about Rosie...'

'Don't worry about it,' Blaze advised, lazily toying with a strand of her hair. 'You'll maybe have worked out your penance by about our sixth child...'

'Our sixth?' she gasped, sitting bolt upright in shock.

A lean hand flattened her back on the pillows. He rolled over and trapped her with the weight of his body. Jewelled eyes, brilliant with amusement, rested on her. 'I plan to keep you very busy in the bedroom...'

MILLION DOLLAR SWEEPSTAKES (III)

No purchase necessary. To enter, follow the directions published. Method of entry may vary. For eligibility, entries must be received no later than March 31, 1996. No liability is assumed for printing errors, lost, late or misdirected entries. Odds of winning are determined by the number of eligible entries distributed and received. Prizewinners will be determined no later than June 30, 1996.

Sweepstakes open to residents of the U.S. (except Puerto Rico), Canada, Europe and Taiwan who are 18 years of age or older. All applicable laws and regulations apply. Sweepstakes offer void wherever prohibited by law. Values of all prizes are in U.S. currency. This sweepstakes is presented by Torstar Corp., its subsidiaries and affiliates, in conjunction with book, merchandise and/or product offerings. For a copy of the Official Rules send a self-addressed, stamped envelope (WA residents need not affix return postage) to: MILLION DOLLAR SWEEPSTAKES (III) Rules, P.O. Box 4573, Blair, NE 68009, USA.

EXTRA BONUS PRIZE DRAWING

No purchase necessary. The Extra Bonus Prize will be awarded in a random drawing to be conducted no later than 5/30/96 from among all entries received. To qualify, entries must be received by 3/31/96 and comply with published directions. Drawing open to residents of the U.S. (except Puerto Rico), Canada, Europe and Taiwan who are 18 years of age or older. All applicable laws and regulations apply; offer void wherever prohibited by law. Odds of winning are dependent upon number of eligibile entries received. Prize is valued in U.S. currency. The offer is presented by Torstar Corp., its subsidiaries and affiliates in conjunction with book, merchandise and/or product offering. For a copy of the Official Rules governing this sweepstakes, send a self-addressed, stamped envelope (WA residents need not affix return postage) to: Extra Bonus Prize Drawing Rules, P.O. Box 4590, Blair, NE 68009, USA.

SWP-H595